Copyright Matthew
Edited b
All rights reserved. N
reproduced in any form c
inclusion of brief quotal
permission in writir

This book is a work of fiction. The characters and situations in this book are imaginary. No resemblance is intended between these characters and any persons, living or dead.

This book is sold subject to the condition that it shall not, by way of trade or otherwise, be lent, resold, hired out or otherwise circulated without the publisher's prior consent in any form or binding or cover other than that in which it is published and without similar condition including this condition being imposed on the subsequent purchaser.

Published in Great Britain in 2022 by Matthew Cash Burdizzo Books Walsall, UK

FERAL

Matthew Cash

FERAL

MATTHEW CASH

FERAL

Prologue

Transfixed by the man sitting on top of the burning mound, Danny watched the melting figure as the flames devoured its flesh. As the fats beneath the splitting skin popped, sizzled, and dripped into the pyre, a bonfire in the literal sense. The smell wasn't entirely unpleasant if you didn't think about what was fuelling the fire.

Despite the heat of the mass cremation, the tip of the gun was ice against the nape of his neck where Tony was pressing the weapon. He focused on the burning bodies and hoped it would be enough.

Stars faded in the sky and Danny thought about fairies and Peter Pan. This view, and the sound of approaching vehicles would be the accompanying soundtrack to the last few moments of his life. "Just do it," he croaked, his voice thick with emotion.

Tony's finger rested on the trigger, memories flooding his mind. Toddlers playing. Children running. A happier time before hormones came along and changed everything.

Cars braked, footsteps raced, and men shouted; he knew it was now or never.

He took one last breath, released it slowly, and wondered if he would have enough time to throw his brother's body on the heap with the others.

FERAL

Part 1

FERAL

Chapter 1

Bartholomew Tepes spotted the kid a mile away; they were as inconspicuous as an explosion at a Christmas Market. It made him chuckle. His slight, doughy jowls trembled above the fastened collar of his German parka as he saw the kid tap something into his mobile phone. They were all the same, but when needs be, beggars couldn't be choosers, oh no.

The youth had long, dyed-black hair, wore thick, pale foundation and dark eyeliner and lipstick, was painfully thin, and had no distinguishing features whatsoever. A doll. It was impossible to tell if they were male or female. And it really didn't matter. These days you got into trouble for 'assuming people's genders.' Bartholomew didn't give two fucks about that kind of thing; as far as he was concerned, there were two types of person: him, and them.

So far, at fifty-five, Bartholomew Tepes hadn't met anyone like himself.

He stalked the teenager closely, having given him a deliberately false description of what he would be wearing— a failsafe, as he didn't trust anyone. Nothing he was doing was technically illegal. Yet. He wasn't some seedy, grooming, perverted paedophile, despite the obvious age gap between him and his potential date. The youth was two years past the age of consent, although not many rational minded people would have consented to Bartholomew's proposals.

The non-gender specific waif tapped a black-varnished fingertip against the screen of something portable and plucked black earbuds from within the dark flow of their ebony hair. The earphones were then secreted in the sagging pockets of a baggy hoodie depicting some Satanic effigy with a band's logo in practically unintelligible font. From out of the same pocket, a cylindrical device was retrieved.

The young and their toys, Bartholomew thought impatiently, and continued to observe vape smoke wafting in the air between them. It was good to get up close and personal before pouncing on them; the element of surprise always brought out their true side.

An extra dense cloud of Parma Violet flavoured vapour hung above the youth's head. Bartholomew waved a calloused hand through it and made his grand entrance.

"Not very vampiric, Lestat2000."

The kid spun around, choking on an intake of sweet vapour, thick tendrils of the stuff coming from their nostrils and mouth as they cursed and swore. A mixture of anger and fear soon changed into embarrassment and confusion as they took in the person they had arranged to meet. "Are you...?"

Ah, Bartholomew thought, *at last, we have confirmation, a male – no doubt about it with a voice that deep.* He interrupted the boy and thrust his hand forward. "I am Bartholomew Tepes."

The boy gingerly reached out his hand and Bartholomew grasped it in both of his, sliding the tips of his index and middle fingers up the sleeve of his hoodie and pushing them against the throb of the boy's pulse. The boy flinched but made no bid to pull away. After a few seconds he smiled reassuringly. "My real name is Lee."

Bartholomew smiled, showing large teeth that were the same shade of orange as pumpkin innards. "Would you prefer to be named after that elusive Anne Rice vampire?"

Lee, Lestat2000, gazed at his shoes like someone at least ten years younger, and embarrassment flushed at the sides of his face between cheekbone and ear, where he had poorly applied his white foundation. His nod was barely perceptible, but Bartholomew noticed it.

"Well then, dear Lestat, let us seize this day, good fiend." He threw back the hood of his green parka and shook out a mane of greying black hair. He felt Lestat's eyes upon him, taking in his appearance. Bartholomew had the darkened aspects of the Romany folk: hair that had once been lustrous black curls had now faded to charcoal grey but had kept its vibrance. He wore several silver loops in his right ear and one through his right nostril. He seemed amused by the boy's reaction. "Am I not what you were expecting?"

Lestat slowly brought the vape pen to his lips and tentatively took a suck, remembering the 'not very vampiric' jibe. "Not really, I mean, I don't know what I was expecting."

"Someone bedecked in Victorian garb akin to Gary Oldman in that dire version of Bram's finest creation, no doubt?" Bartholomew guessed. All this lot were the same, thought they knew it all, but they only followed trends and movie icons.

Lestat shrugged. "I guess I expected that someone who reckons that they are a true vampire would at least dress like one."

The comment was meant to be bitchy, maybe even clever, but Bartholomew found it hilarious; his laughter was raucous and startled passers-by. "Boy, why must we be walking advertisements for what we are? Do you want everyone to know that you are a vampire? Is that it?" The older man smiled at several shoppers and addressed one middle-aged couple. "He's a vampire, don't you know?"

The couple glanced at one another, laughed politely, and quickened their pace.

Lestat turned to hide his face against a shop window. "Fuck's sake." He felt one of Bartholomew's strong hands clamp down on his shoulder, raised his head, and used the reflection to look at the man.

Bartholomew smiled warmly into the glass, ignoring the bakery produce behind it, and focused only on the stooped-over young man. A lady in the bakery smiled and waved at him; he pointed at the produce on display and rubbed his belly with a grin. "You see, Lee, our kind has been around since the dawn of Mankind, but the successful ones are those who learn camouflage; learn how to blend in and hide away, dust over any footprints they may leave in the snow." With that, he vanished into the shop.

Lestat, no, *Lee,* Lee understood what Bartholomew was trying to tell him, hence all the secrecy in their meeting, a town undisclosed until twenty-four hours before, a rendezvous point to be confirmed once they had both arrived at the destination. No one must know about this liaison. The app they had met on was completely anonymous, too, but Lee had done as requested: he had sent Bartholomew photographs of himself. He regretted that now, but knew it had been part of the deal, part of the trust, so that he could be found. Bartholomew said he liked to keep a close watch on his children but not the other way around. This was the real deal, Lee knew it, he could tell just by how different this man was; the others had been childish in comparison. A recollection of a video running the circuits on social media sprang to mind, a man and woman who were old enough to be his parents wearing loads of goth gear, wannabe Marilyn Mansons, who claimed to be real vampires. They drank each other's blood in wine glasses and wore funereal clothing, and at the time Lee had felt as though his eyes had been opened. Being a vampire was not an image, a trend, it really was a way of life for some people.

Act normally and fit in, be a successful vampire.

Bartholomew materialised out of the shop doorway, paper bags clutched in his hands. "Sausage rolls. I take it you're not vegetarian. Need to get your blood up."

FERAL

Chapter 2

Chaos.
Cacophony.
Sirens, emergency vehicles of every kind.

Juliet paused as an army truck sped past, missing her by inches. Attacks were happening all over the town. The hospital, the police station, a nursery, and the park.

Something evil had come to Boxford and all she wanted was her children and her father. The shock of the night's events was slowly sinking in. The old German sliding a blade into her boyfriend's head as he lay comatose in the hospital, followed by a brief apology before he hurled himself through a double-glazed window, seven storeys high, seemingly unscathed.

The news reports said *werewolves*, but they'd thrown the word around lightly, as though it was only temporary until they found out what was really going on.

Werewolves, the creatures of nightmares and horror films.

She had seen the strange CCTV footage of what appeared to be a monster in the lift of her father's apartment block. And the grainy footage from the hospital the night six people were slaughtered. It was impossible, but no other explanations were forthcoming.

Swarms of police buzzed around the Green Man Estate. The five tower blocks were surrounded by an array of official vehicles. Rows of police officers kept a huge crowd of pyjama-clad residents at bay. Juliet rushed through the excited onlookers as they watched armed men enter each building in turn. She scanned people's faces, searching for her father and children.

A woman she vaguely recognised was sitting on the step of an ambulance, huddled in a blanket, talking to a police officer. "Excuse me, I need to speak to someone about my children. They're in that building."

The officer waved to one of the other officers near the cordon and spoke into her radio.

Juliet looked across the car park as the other officer checked a clipboard and shook his head.

"What the bloody hell does that mean?" she asked.

"It means they are still in the flats, or were somewhere else when all this kicked off," the WPC replied, before patting the blanketed woman on the shoulder and walking away.

"They're finding it all very hard to believe," the woman said, her glazed-over expression telling Juliet she was reliving something she would rather not.

"What happened?" Juliet blurted out, still scanning the people.

"Them fucking things on the telly, that's what," the woman said with a hollow laugh, "fucking werewolves."

There was that word again. "I know you, don't I?"

The woman nodded. "Yeah, I'm Bex. I work in the café at the supermarket."

"You know my dad, then, Trevor? I'm trying to find him; he's babysitting my kids."

Bex's eyes went wide and she slid off the ambulance and landed on her feet, the blanket falling to the tarmac. "Oh, dear God," she whispered in a tiny voice.

Juliet's face mirrored Bex's look of horror and she spun around, her handbag thwacking against Bex's outreached hand as she reached out to stop her from leaving the ambulance. Juliet raced towards the looming grey tower block wishing herself already at her father's flat.

"Wait," said one of the police officers, stepping between Juliet and the main entrance, "we're not allowing anyone in until we've checked all the properties."

"Please, my father and children are in there," she cried, trying to edge her way past.

The officer beckoned to his female colleague. "Will you accompany this lady to her father's flat? Jimmy said all the floors have been searched up to the seventh floor—"

"That's my dad's floor! My kids are up there!" Juliet interrupted and shoulder-barged the policeman out of the way.

"Go with her," she heard the male officer shout as she made for the entrance.

People in white coveralls milled around in the ground floor lobby, snapping photographs of blood pools and spatter-patterns; she turned away from them and pushed through the door to the stairwell.

The WPC caught up with her as she pounded up the first flight of stairs, joining in with her panicked run. On the third floor, Juliet paused, her heart thudding in her chest; she never had been one for physical exertion.

"Look, just slow down a bit, yeah?" the WPC suggested. "There's officers everywhere."

"They'll be okay, won't they?" Juliet asked. They *had* to be okay; they just had to. Whatever was going on around here couldn't have anything to do with her dad. The man she had known all her life was kind and gentle and loving; she wouldn't have left her kids with him otherwise—

FERAL

She stopped as her mind replayed the scene from the night before, the German killing her boyfriend and then hurtling through the window like something out of one of the superhero films Kiran liked to watch. *Kiran.* His little face flashed before her eyes: the cute little bow of his mouth, the enormous Disney eyes, and those chubby cheeks that dimpled whenever he smiled.

Juliet resumed climbing the stairs and the game Kayleigh used to play sprang to mind, a silly game that she would never admit was extremely annoying. When she went up any stairs she would sing some nursery rhyme or other that she had heard in the playground. With each step she took, she assigned it a letter, and at the top of her lungs, in an American accent, she would sing, "A-B-C-D and E, I love you, my mummy." Juliet thought it sounded like something from that programme her eldest two—Jamal and Jeanelle—used to watch, that cringeworthy purple T-Rex; that would account for the American accent.

"A-B-C-D and E, I love you, my mummy."

As annoying as it would get, especially when the lifts were out and it would be repeated every half-dozen steps, right now, she hoped and prayed that she would get to hear it again.

Juliet burst from the stairwell and banged hard on her father's front door. No answer. Without hesitation she swung her handbag in front of her and started rifling through it for the spare set of keys she kept there in case of emergency. She half-expected to hear the elderly Jamaican's voice whining as he rushed up the hallway. "What's all this commotion?" he would say, his face screwed up in concern—which would no doubt turn to surprise when he saw Juliet with a police escort.

He'd let them in; Kiran and Kayleigh would probably be lounging on his threadbare settee watching CBeebies, and they would sit in the kitchen drinking coffee and talking about the previous night's events. Knowing her dad, he would be oblivious to how corrupt his old German friend was, a lot of the world's most evil of men were experts at hiding in plain sight. None of it made sense and she doubted her dad would be able to shed any more light on the matter.

She found the keys, three silver and one brass, with a scratched plastic keyring depicting the flag of Jamaica. Her hand shook as she tried to fit the first key in the bottom lock.

"May I?" the police officer asked.

Juliet handed over the keys.

"What's your dad's name, love?"

"Trevor."

"Okay." She pressed her ear against the door. "Hello, Trevor? I'm WPC Davies, I'm with your daughter and we've come to see if you are alright."

The bottom of the door grated against the floor and PC Davies noted that the wood around the lock was splintered and cracked. It was a sign of trouble and she immediately barked information into the radio on her chest. "Hello, this is WPC Davies, on the seventh floor. We have a break-in at number —"

Juliet pushed the police officer out of the way and ran into her father's flat.

"No, wait!" the WPC cried, "it might not be safe!" But it was too late: Juliet was in.

FERAL

Chapter 3

"Run," Tony said, it was a bossy older brother's demand. He thrust his hand under Danny's arm, grabbed his bicep and pushed him toward the bonfire. For a second Danny thought his brother was going to shove him face-first into the flames and he gave no resistance. But Tony pulled him in the direction of a small path to the left of the fire. As they passed the mass funeral pyre Tony flung the gun into the furnace.

"I said run," he spat petrified and dragged him through a gap in a hedge.

A cottage sat on the edge of the park, the Scarborough boys had admired its large garden and swimming pool ever since they were small and their mum was still alive. Now they crept through the rising fog amongst the dew grubby, bloody, and exhausted past a teardrop-shaped swimming pool. Sirens wailed in the dawn air and not too far away they heard the buzzing of a helicopter.

"Why the hell didn't you just pull the damn trigger?" Danny whispered as Tony yanked him behind a garden shed.

"Why the hell do you think?" Tony hissed and froze as one of the lights upstairs in the house came on. A shadow passed the window.

"What are we going to do?" Danny whined; he was beginning to sound like he had when they were younger.

Tony ignored his questions and did something on his phone.

The wound on Danny's arm had stopped bleeding altogether now. That was worrying for how deep it had been. Danny knew what it meant; he was going to turn into one of those things.

An eternity passed as they crouched behind the garden shed, the day got brighter and the police activity in the park got louder. Nobody came out of the house. It was still too early for most people to get up.

"We need to get to Sudbury, there's somewhere we can stay," Tony said calmly. He nodded to a red car that was beside the house. "I don't suppose you picked up any tricks from hanging around with the GMC, did you?"

Danny smirked sheepishly. "One or two, but busting into a car's one thing, getting started is another entirely. They make it look easy in the films but it's not, especially with all the modern locks and stuff."

Tony sighed but knew it would just add another thing to the growing list of trouble they were already in. He had his mobile phone, knew there was no money in his wallet and next to nothing in his bank account. Payday was another fortnight away as if that held any relevance.

"I think we're going to have to do an Über bunk."

Before his younger brother could confirm or protest this suggestion Tony tapped details into an app on his phone.

The Über bunk was something people had done since the dawn of time, or at least since the dawn of public taxi services. There were endless variations, they came under many guises, and were called different things but they all had one thing in common; to swindle the driver out of a free ride. Until taxi drivers began to insist on payment upfront for all fares this would never stop.

Waiting for the car to come seemed to take hours even though he suspected it was all in his mind. Tony wanted to hide from every approaching vehicle, sure it would be the police. Eventually, a blue Mondeo came rolling down the narrow road towards the house, loud Indian music blaring out into the morning air. A wrinkled prune of a man in a skullcap nodded sombrely at them, turned the volume down on the radio and simply asked. "Sudbury?"

They got in the car.

The driver sped along the quiet side roads but slowed when he hit the busier main ones.

"Lots of police about this morning?" the taxi driver said, eyes flicking at Tony in the rear-view mirror in what looked like mild suspicion.

"Yeah," Tony mumbled noncommittally, never taking his eyes from the passing vehicles.

"Trouble in the Arboretum, init? A load of bloody weirdos acting like it's Halloween still." The taxi driver shook his head and tutted.

"That's Boxford."

"You two Boxford boys?"

The brothers exchanged glances, Tony said something to shut down the conversation. "No, we're going home, we came to see some friends last night. Turns out the locals here don't like gay people. They seem to turn against anything that dares to be different."

The taxi driver nodded slowly and spent the rest of the journey silent.

Chapter 4

They kept firing, the soldiers.

Mortimer knew from the minute the old fat man's feet slapped the tarmac that he himself would be collateral, that the old man's capture, alive or dead, was paramount. Bullets entered Herbert without him even registering, fortunately hitting nowhere important. A flashback from the old black-and-white King Kong sprang to mind as he hung in the thing's grasp, one of its chunky arms looped over the high wire fence, the razor barbs curling into the pale pink flesh. The monster's face contorted back into that of a portly old man as he shouted for him to stop, let him go, that they wanted a live specimen. It had been stupid; *he* had been stupid. The old man would rather be killed than subjected to more of his torturous experimentation and that's what would happen if he were to be recaptured.

"Please, Herbert," he cried, gazing up to the pale, distorted head, "I know you can hear me, let me go, give yourself up, they want a live specimen."

The flesh and the muscles around the monster's pointed snout melted away and the vague semblance of the man beneath growled in hatred. "Then you can be it!" He thrust his fat neck against the rusted razor wire and tore out his own throat.

Blood sprayed from the jagged ruin below the man-monster's chin and Mortimer felt himself being lifted higher in the crook of the man's elbow, and he face-planted that gushing wound.

Blood filling his mouth and nostrils, he grabbed fistfuls of the old man's hospital gown and tried to push himself away. He felt a hot jet of plasma fire down the back of his throat and began to choke. He instinctively swallowed.

Herbert threw him away from the top of the fence and for a moment he flew through the air before he landed hard on the bonnet of one of the military jeeps, his back snapping and his head smashing one of the headlights.

Mortimer's mind was a whir of confusion. Faces and events both real and imaginary plagued his unconscious as he lay in the facility. Towards the end of his brief liaison skirting the thoroughfare between life and death, he was suddenly aware of pain. Deep within his skull, he felt something twitch, squirm, and send electrical pulses to the pinpoints of agony throughout his body. Most of the damage had been fixed whilst he was firmly wrapped in the blanketing embrace of the coma, so now it was time for them to bring him round and test the outer layers of his perception.

Mortimer opened his eyes and immediately groaned at the brightness of the strip lighting above. He was lying flat out on a bed, with only a thin sheet covering his modesty. "Oh fuck," he said in a hoarse whisper as the realisation hit.

He was at the facility at the barracks, the special facility where he had tried to find out everything about the monster that had escaped; if it *had* escaped, that was. Groggily, he forced himself up onto his elbows and was only half-surprised to see his fat eastern European assistant sitting on the other side of the small room, his doughy buttocks spilling over the sides of the swivel chair. Gustav had his back to the bed as he tapped away at a computer keyboard, a plate of sandwiches on the desk. The man was forever eating.

FERAL

Mortimer cleared his throat and watched as Gustav tapped away for a few more seconds before he spun around on the chair and regarded him with a stony face and a hint of tedium. Without offering a word, he spun back around, grabbed a triangular sandwich in one hand and a mobile phone in the other. After quickly taking a mouthful, he pressed a button on the handset, pushed the food to the side of his mouth and muttered into the phone. "Sir Jonathan, he's awake."

*

Sir Jonathan Butcher lowered the sleek black smartphone onto a paper-covered table next to his chair and closed his eyes. A smile, an alien thing upon his decrepit, bitter face, made the heavy lines set into the corners of his lips twitch upward.

He resembled something both avian and human spliced together. Pale skin covered his scalp; with his hooked beak of a nose and his spindly, degenerating limbs, it was as though he were a human fledgeling turfed out of the nest to freeze and wither on the ground.

He flopped his arm uselessly and allowed a moment or two for numerous toxins to enter his body intravenously, that they might participate in the seemingly endless battle against the great black poison spreading inside him. *Cancer* rhymed with *dancer* and *prancer* and those things were exactly what it was doing inside Sir Jonathan's organs, flitting from one to the next, fleetingly touching everything with its dark, dripping fingertips.

His smile faltered as he cast his eyes over the network of scars across his pigeon chest and swollen belly and hoped to Christ that there would be enough time left. Sir Jonathan wasn't a religious man; he had absolute faith that death was the end and had spent most of his adult life trying to ward it off. He knew he would be lucky to last another month but felt certain now that the end of his suffering was at hand. The events from the shabby dead-end town had been witnessed across the globe, with more details being added by the hour.

The latest updates pleased him,. Yes, they had lost their captured live specimen, but against all expectations, the captive had headed straight back to Boxford and finished off his friends in a melee of destruction. Police were looking for two young men after finding a heap of smouldering corpses in the town's vast park. It was messy, all so messy, but it was a mess that could be cleaned up. Sir Jonathan would see to it that some elaborately woven cloth be draped over the whole matter as soon as possible. And they still had a captured specimen, unfortunately not as mature as the escapee, but nevertheless, Sir Jonathan eyed the chemotherapy apparatus set up around him, musing that *beggars can't be choosers.*

A wave of nauseating pain screwed his rotting stomach up and made the old man lurch forward, his breath catching in his chest. He thumbed at a red alarm button on the armrest. Two officials in white uniforms and a young man in a brown suit rushed into the room and did what they could to comfort him.

FERAL

Chapter 5
1945

"You were very lucky," Victor heard the familiar voice say as his vision began to clear. Liebermann hovered over him, a silhouette beneath the overhead lighting. "My men managed to miss your vital organs."

He remembered. They had shot them both: he and his wife. "Gwen?" His chest was agony, fire, discernible even beneath whatever concoction they had dosed him with.

Liebermann swam in and out of focus. "I'm afraid she wasn't so fortunate."

Victor closed his eyes. At least she would be at peace now. He would be with her soon enough.

"Once you have told me everything you know about your work, then you can join her," Liebermann said, as though reading his mind. "Until then, you are going nowhere."

"Where is my wife?" Victor kept his eyes closed so the SS commander wouldn't see the fear.

"She is buried a few kilometres from here. When you are well enough to recreate the work you destroyed, I will have you taken to her, and if you so wish, I will even bury you alongside." Liebermann blurred and doubled in Victor's vision.

Victor fluttered a hand towards him. "Get me a journal and a pen and I'll begin as soon as I can see clearly."

Liebermann grinned maliciously. "Good, Victor, good. You'll be with her soon, I'm sure."

FERAL

When Victor awoke the next morning he knew he had made a grave mistake. He wondered what the consequences would be. He felt too good; he shouldn't even be alive, let alone conscious. One of Liebermann's trusted goons, a heavy-set man named Ferdinand, held vigil over him. Victor was of high value despite the absolute betrayal he had shown them, and they were determined he would live. There was no way out.

He began recreating his notes as soon as he could sit up. Victor knew his rapid recovery would be investigated if he didn't at least appear frailer than he was, but he knew his time was limited. If what he had learned from the Schäfer family was correct, and he believed they had told him the truth, then he would have until the next full moon. He had to be away from these men by then.

His studies had shown that the Schäfer family's condition was nothing short of miraculous: their regenerative capabilities, their longevity, their strength. Victor had noted a trio of weaknesses: silver; fire, only if fierce and constant; and what could only be described as internal struggle, where the victim would battle long and hard with the beast within themselves, more often than not, succumbing.

Something the father had said echoed in his mind, something he had kept out of the previous journal. "No matter whether you are born Lycan or have turned, no matter if you have total control over your wolf for all your life, give it the chance and it will rise to the surface in a heartbeat and take over just like that. It is a wild beast. Always a wild beast. It can never, ever, be fully tamed." The big man's wicked grin had glinted in the bush of his red beard like a blade in a pile of autumn leaves. He had known exactly what Victor and the Nazi party were up to.

Victor made his notes, recreated diagrams and mathematical formulas from memory, and gave an accurate retelling of the family's history. It needed to be convincing. Even if he gave them the truth, it would be useless now the Schäfers were all dead. As far as Liebermann was concerned, they were the last of their kind. That was why Victor needed to escape. Things were different now.

Victor hoped Liebermann was telling the truth about Gwen, that she was buried nearby. The last he had seen of her had been when Liebermann had had his men open fire. He had no idea how the lycanthropy would affect her, wherever she was. Surely, if she were alive, they would have said so, anything to use against him. He had images of her buried alive in a shallow grave. Would the unnatural elixir in her body repair her, even below several feet of soil, or would she repeatedly resuscitate and suffocate until somebody dug her up, or would the thing inside her become too weak and give up the fight?

*

After a few days into his convalescence, Victor began to play the part of the cantankerous old man. Up until then, he had been compliant for the doctors and nurses, but as he started feeling stronger, he started a tiresome tirade against the medical staff. He belittled them, verbally abused them, and refused both examination and medication. Force was used on numerous occasions, and after much of this bad behaviour, Liebermann was sent for, exactly as Victor had planned. The recreation of his journal was almost complete.

At first, he bent truths and fabricated wildly; there was no way they could expect him to remember everything word for word, but in the end he saw no reason to carry on lying. If anything, it was a chance for the old man to gloat in the evil bastards' faces. He would show them exactly what they had had within their grasp and how he had taken it all away from them in one foul, death-filled afternoon.

Aside from him, the only evidence in the world that this abnormality existed was his wife's dead body. He furiously told them everything he knew, wanting it over as quickly as possible. If Liebermann didn't keep to his word, then so help him and the rest of them come full moon.

Like an over-excited child, Liebermann snatched the journal from his hand.

"I don't know what you hope to gain from this," Victor said softly. "There is no possible way you can recreate this. The Schäfers were all killed, their bodies destroyed by fire."

Liebermann's grin widened. "Did you really think you were the only one conducting experiments, Victor?"

The bottom fell out of Victor's world; deflated, his head shook involuntary. "No!"

Liebermann laughed. "You murdered those children for nothing. The experiments had already begun."

"No," Victor said, suddenly feeling age creeping back into his bones.

Inside him, something new prickled its ears, but it was not mature enough yet for its debut performance.

"But this will be most useful," Liebermann said, tapping the journal with a finger. "I thank you, Victor Krauss, you may have helped the Führer win this war after all. Eat well tonight, for tomorrow, I shall take you to your wife."

Victor didn't sleep.

Visions of a hungry horde of werewolf soldiers, brainwashed beneath the Nazi flag, flooded his thoughts. A new world order, and he had done nothing to prevent it. The only consolation was that it would soon be over, for him at least. If they didn't do it, he would do it himself.

Maybe it was divine intervention, or bad luck, on Liebermann's part, but that night, the sky was torn apart with thunder and fire.

The British were bombing them.

Victor was the only one in the hospital who wasn't scared.

In the morning, Liebermann, dishevelled and battle-scarred, stormed into the room, grabbed him by the throat, and threw him across the room, a Mauser against his forehead. "It's all gone!" he spat, the gun digging into his skin, "all fucking gone."

Victor was too shaken at first by the sudden physical onslaught to comprehend what Liebermann meant, but the fabric strengthening him from the inside was making him more resilient.

Victor smiled up at the Nazi bastard welcoming his own death. He nodded to the Mauser and pressed his head against the cold metal. "Do it, Liebermann. What are you waiting for?"

The fury dissipated from the Nazi's face and he lowered the gun. "I may as well point it at my own head. I think I'll just let you die an old man." He sighed and reholstered the weapon. "Who knows what things the Schäfers' secrets could have done to help others, Victor?

They could have done you a lot of good. This was one of the greatest medical discoveries, the gift of regeneration. You could have lived forever. Imagine that."

"I have lived long enough. It was unnatural; the Schäfers knew that, that's why they lived in exile, to keep it away from the likes of you. It was meant to die with them, and so it has."

"Maybe. It makes no difference now." Liebermann glazed over, and handed Victor a folded sheet of paper, bearing a crude but intelligible map. "I'm a man of my word, Victor Krauss, and you kept your part of the bargain even though you did betray us all first." The Nazi backed away towards the door and smiled sadly at Victor's confusion. "That's where your wife is buried."

The next morning, Victor was awoken by Liebermann's man, Ferdinand, and another soldier, and given twenty minutes to gather his things and dress. *This is it,* Victor thought, and imagined a firing squad waiting at dawn. He did as instructed and was led outside for the first time in what felt like weeks. Physically, he felt like someone fifty years younger, but mentally he was prepared for death.

He was ushered towards an open-top jeep, his bag slung into the back seat beside him. The two soldiers rode up front.

As the jeep pulled away from the hospital, Victor saw the devastation the British had wrought on the nearby headquarters. Buildings that had once stood erect with a cold, grey grandeur were reduced to rubble. People picked through the debris like vultures. War was horrible, but at least this bombing had put an end to a terrible regime that might have destroyed most of civilisation.

Victor let the ruins of the block that had once housed his laboratory pass by and couldn't help but wonder what gruesome things Liebermann had already brought to fruition before its destruction.

The base was on the outskirts of a small, picturesque town, a number of its houses in ruins. He pitied the innocent lives that had been lost. The jeep sped through the town towards a dirt track which ran amidst tall pines and wound up a steep incline over the crest of the valley. The sun seeped over the mountainous horizon, slowly bringing warmth to the dip in the German countryside. Victor squinted as rays shone in his eyes. They drove for a further three miles, climbing to the valley's summit. Below, mist rose from the valley, all but obscuring the little town.

"Just up here," Ferdinand said to the young soldier behind the wheel. He pointed to a layby at the side of the track, where a large log-pile sat.

"Out," Ferdinand ordered, and held the door open for Victor.

"Liebermann sent you to do his dirty work, then?" Victor said, casually picking up his bag, all that remained of his life with Gwen.

"Quiet, Krauss," Ferdinand spat, and began to roll a cigarette.

Avoiding eye contact with Victor, the accompanying soldier reached behind him and retrieved a shovel.

Ferdinand led the procession through the pine forest, keeping the log-pile behind them. The young soldier brought up the rear, shovel tucked under one arm, rifle pointed into the stooping back of the ninety-year-old in front of him.

FERAL

Victor panted and wheezed with physical exertion, although it was mostly for show. Even before he had infected himself with lycanthropy he had been considerably agile. "Please," he said, trying his best to sound his age and letting his bag slip from his grasp, "how much further?"

"Five minutes," Ferdinand said over his shoulder.

Victor sighed and gestured a shaking hand to his bag. "Please, sir, could you?"

Ferdinand sneered and struck a boot out at his belongings. "Leave it. I'll have him throw it in with you before we bury you."

Victor's lower lip trembled, which seemed to heighten Ferdinand's delight. "Very well. Please do that."

The morbid fanfare continued for another few minutes until they came to a clearing. Ferdinand, ten feet ahead, stepped into it before Victor and shouted in alarm. Victor instantly quickened his pace, the soldier behind matched him.

Victor saw past Ferdinand into the clearing at the misshapen hole in the ground. He quit the old man act and allowed the inner exuberance he had been feeling to rush to the surface. If this was where they had buried Gwen, there was a chance she was still alive. He acted quickly.

He lunged for the young soldier, the only one with his weapon drawn, but instead of reaching for the rifle he snatched the handle sticking out from underneath his armpit. He swung the shovel around as hard and as fast as he could into Ferdinand's face, knocking him to the ground.

The young soldier, only beginning to realise what was happening, was amazed at how quick the doddery old man had sprung at him. He aimed his gun but was too late.

Victor thrust the handle of the shovel against the bridge of the soldier's nose.

The soldier grunted as the bone shattered and he lost consciousness.

The rifle dropped to the ground. Victor picked it up and stood between the two, gun in one hand, shovel in the other, and watched as both comatose men began to move. He raised the rifle.

The young soldier sat up at the sound of the gunshot and the moist splatter of Ferdinand's brains across his cheeks. He looked at Victor, a mere frightened child.

"I'm sorry for breaking your nose," Victor said, raising the rifle once more, lining it up with the young man's face before realising he didn't have to be a monster too. "Now, go. Tell them what happened."

The soldier leapt up and ran unsteadily through the pines.

Victor went to look for his wife.

FERAL

Chapter 6

Juliet's knees gave out at the first sight of red.

Dark arterial blood, black in the half-light of the hall, streaked the magnolia walls and glossy doors. She tried to call out for her dad but something huddled at the end of the passage stole her breath.

Her eyes adjusted to the gloom.

Two shapes beneath a blanket.

"Juliet!" It was the policewoman who had followed her. "Come back out with me."

"I need to see." Juliet forced the words out and staggered towards the end of the hallway.

"No, no. Let's wait for the others to get here, you might accidentally disturb something important. Evidence." The WPC held her back, though she knew it was futile. "Stay here, please."

Juliet stopped.

The officer switched the lights on.

"Oh my God, there's so much blood," Juliet moaned, in turmoil about what her father might have done. To his own grandchildren.

"Stay there," the officer said, sternly this time, and walked over to the blanket that was blocking Juliet's view from whatever lay beneath.

She pulled back the cover.

Two children, a boy and a girl, strikingly similar, lay huddled against each other. Apart from scraps of nightwear, they were naked, their skin covered in dried blood and clumps of gore, just like the floor around them.

The police officer couldn't see any physical injuries on either child. The boy's chest rose and fell with a shallow hitch, and the girl's mouth twitched at the corners, as though she were dreaming.

"They're alive!" The police officer laughed in disbelief.

Juliet stumbled down the hallway, her hands clamped over her mouth at the sight of her sleeping crimson babies.

Kiran and Kayleigh were horror movie props, sleeping satanic cherubim in a patch of dried blood, which, unbeknownst to her, was all their own.

The next twenty minutes went by in a blur of yellow-jacketed officers.

Her children were wrapped in blankets and rushed to awaiting ambulances.

She sat with them in a state of shock, not knowing if any of this was even real.

The only thing that mattered was the fogs of breath inside their oxygen masks.

Everything else could wait.

Her head was a flurry of thoughts.
What's Dad involved in?
Is it just the old German guy who's corrupt or has he roped Dad into it, too? Is it drugs?
It all points towards drugs.
She had heard tales of pensioners touting their prescription drugs to make money, or faking ailments to get high-strength painkillers and then sell them illegally.
It must be something like that.
Monsters aren't real.
The only monsters around here walked with two legs and bled red. No one would tell her anything but already she was piecing the parts together.

If somehow Krauss had been the one funding the local hoodlums, and her father had become involved and things turned nasty, she would never forgive him.

How many times had he endangered her children?

His grandchildren.

In her mind, she saw images of masked thugs breaking into his flat to make him pay.

But what about my kids?
Would they have hurt them, too?
Would he have protected them with his life?
Dad must have known whoever it was that knocking.

A wave of unanswerable questions threatened to flood Juliet's mind as she sat in the deserted hospital waiting room. She thought of her children: a nurse had come in just thirty minutes earlier to say they were fine but still unconscious, and that she would be able to see them once they had run a few more tests.

The police officer and a colleague had been in to ask her the same questions about her dad and the Green Man Crew. They asked her several times if she had heard anything about a new drug in the area, as they had discovered a vial containing unknown toxins.

Juliet knew nothing about any drug. All she cared about were her babies and finding out how her father was involved in all of this. She cradled her face in her hands, the weight of everything forcing her to tears.

David, too. She had finally found a decent man, after all those bloody years, and Victor Krauss had killed him without hesitation.

She wondered how much more she would have to endure before she woke up from all this.

"Hi, Juliet," came a soft voice. It was the nurse again. She stood timidly in the doorway. "I'm sorry if you were resting."

Juliet sprang up, automatically expecting the worst. "What's happened? Oh my god, what's happened?"

"It's okay, it's okay. They're okay. That's what I've come to tell you. Kiran and Kayleigh. They've woken up."

Chapter 7

The problem was, he felt great. That's how he knew whatever was in the old man was now inside him, too.

How remarkable this thing was.

It was why they had all wanted it.

Mortimer felt the anxiety of a future filled with restraints, dissection, and experimentation, buffered by a woollen warmth, something new and alien. Something inside, which hadn't been there before Herbert bled into him like a vampire.

It eased his worries without uttering a word of reassurance, gave him faith that he would find a way to escape.

Let them run their tests, it's only pain.
Pain is just weakness leaving the body.

He remembered something a strict—and completely irrational—personal trainer had said when he was younger. *It's only pain, it won't hurt.*

They still had his notes on the old man, Herbert; he had torn that man apart and watched as he repaired himself.

Everything had already been documented —and well.

Maybe they could work together on this?

The only part of the old man he didn't pry open was his skull.

Even though he desperately wanted to crack it open to see how this thing worked, he knew it was too valuable to destroy if they had only the one specimen. Herbert's escape had proven fruitful for Butcher and the facility; they had irrefutable proof that lycanthropy could be passed on through blood transfusion, and that it took effect rapidly. They already had his notes on its regenerative capabilities.

The next step would see them breed from it so they could try to find out what lay inside the brain.

He had to prove his value. He had to show Butcher he was too important to die.

*

Sir Jonathan Butcher's private ambulance rushed down the motorway. Two nurses hovered around the frail chick in the nest of wires, his eyes burning with furious resilience. Hanging inches from his face was a triple screen, showing GPS of the ambulance's journey, a live reading of his vitals, and a list of phone contacts. "Call Gustav," Butcher wheezed into a pinprick microphone at the base of the screen.

A small box popped up showing his decrepit face as a video call was dialling. His man at the facility had tried to phone him directly as the nurses were transferring him to the ambulance. Whatever news Gustav had, it must have been important. If Mortimer had died, Butcher would have the fat imbecile shot.

The Ukrainian answered immediately and was unusually animated. This was significant; he rarely showed any emotion.

"What is it?" Butcher whispered from behind the oxygen mask.

"Sir, we've had word from Sudbury General. They've had two survivors from Boxford."

The green digits of Butcher's pulse rose half a dozen numbers. The last thing they needed was more witnesses.

So far, the newspapers had been fooled by convincing tales of gang warfare: the Green Man Crew and a rival gang from Sudbury at war on the streets of the small town. All talk of monsters was slowly being abolished from the press. There were people searching for the missing members of the gang, and most had been dealt with.

"Sir Jonathan?"

"Who are the survivors?"

"It's two children, the Jamaican man's grandchildren. They were found in his flat in a pool of blood and gore but there wasn't a scratch on them."

"My God. Is there news from the park? Have we found anything?"

"Nothing but a mound of burning bodies."

"Any sign of the Scarborough boys?"

"No, but we've got the same team looking for them who found the rest of the gang. The police, too. They have been told that they were the main instigators, that it was the gang who broke the younger brother from the police station."

"What about connections to the old people?"

"There wasn't a lot to tidy up. The only one with a child was the Jamaican, and there's nothing we can do about her at the moment as she's surrounded by the police."

Butcher thought of her statement, about seeing Victor Krauss put a blade into a police officer's skull before jumping from a hospital window. He'd read it before he had it destroyed. It didn't erase the information from the woman, however.

Yet another loose end.

Although his body was failing him, his mind was on constant alert. "Kill the mother but bring her children to the facility."

FERAL

Chapter 8

Tony hated that the only person he could go to was him. But they needed money, he had no other choice. They were accomplices to the old woman's murder in the supermarket and the events of the night previous meant they needed to disappear.

Tony knew using his phone would be a risk and also if he were to access his near-empty bank account. At home, in his father's flat, which would be well out of bounds now, swarming with police, there was just over a grand stashed in his bedroom. His plans of escaping Boxford when he had saved enough were over and now he didn't know what was around the corner. He hated the small-minded, dead-end town and wanted to go somewhere bigger. Working at the supermarket café had not been his sole source of income, up until recent events took over his spare time Tony was a sex-worker. His pimp never referred to him by such a term, preferred terms like 'children of the night,' or 'night flyer.' He thought he was the Prince of fucking Darkness like Ozzy Osbourne, but Tony knew what he was and knew no matter how much you tried to glamourise it he sold himself for sexual favours.

Tony succumbed to this murky world after meeting a well-dressed handsome stranger in a wine bar. The man was frivolous with money, plied him with the most expensive of drinks, was well-spoken, intelligent, funny, charming even and then rather than wasting any more time bewitching him, asked Tony to perform fellatio on him for a certain amount of money. Tony was shocked and disgusted, hadn't thought the man serious but ten minutes later he was in the gentleman's toilets with him nonetheless.

The man kept his word and had doubled what he said he would pay him; it was more than he earnt at the café in a week. He gave Tony his card, said if there was anything he needed or wanted, to call him, there were always people he knew who would appreciate boys like him. They might even pay more if he were to be more adventurous, more accommodating. All Tony had to do was call.

Afterwards Tony felt sick, disgusted at what he had done, but the thick wad of cash in his pocket was good compensation for the thick wad of trash he had willingly swallowed. He knew what the man was, screwed the card up and threw it away, but not before storing the number on his phone. Just in case. Just in case he needed to make some more money. He lasted a week. Only one week. A week of enduring existence in a shit hole town with a drunkard whale of a father and a teenage hoodlum for a brother, in a job that was going nowhere serving geriatrics who, though endearing, grew tedious with their repetitive one-liners and unfunny banter. Just one week before he caved in and called him. He was a weaver of words, as tempting as the Devil. Prices were discussed and all money would go through him. It was safer that way, some of the clients could turn nasty and he was Tony's protection. But Tony would be paid handsomely for his work and there was always extra to be earnt for conscientious, young lads who could keep quiet and help others at the drop of a hat. That was how he put it over the phone, his deep suggestive laughter lecherous poison. Tony agreed, at the time he didn't fear the man, he withheld his number and hadn't given him any traceable information, he could bow out any time he wanted. A few weeks, that's all he thought he would have to endure, then he would have enough money to leave Boxford for good. But Tony hadn't known how much Bartholomew Tepes would take, just how much of a gluttonous vampire he was.

*

The taxi pulled up outside a baker's, pet shop and bank, early morning shoppers had joined the throng of commuters. Danny took his card from his wallet and pushed it into the ATM. The machine refused to accept it because it was his library card. Danny threw his arms up in the air and looked back over his shoulder at Tony.

"Fuck sake," Tony muttered under his breath, "it's his turn to pay!" He wound down the window. "What's up?"

"Machine won't accept my card." Danny pushed the card at the slot once more to no avail.

Tony swore again. "Get back in here and let me get some out." He motioned to the taxi driver to unlock the automatic locks, waited for Danny to walk around to the rear of the car before saying to the driver. "Never get with anyone younger than you, mate. They bleed you dry."

The driver smiled uncomfortably. Danny climbed into the car to Tony's right and Tony exited by the left side door.

Tony got to the cash machine and plucked Danny's library card from its slot. "You forgot this, you dickhead," he said and flicked the card at the car.

"Bitch," Danny yelled as the plastic card bounced off the door window and landed in the gutter, he leant out of the taxi as if to retrieve his card and then they both ran.

"When you said there was somewhere to stay I wasn't expecting this," Danny said looking at the semi-detached. Metal shutters covered the windows and doors. A plaque, high up on the fascia between it and the one next-door told him it was called Diana Villas. The whole street was the same, a row of houses waiting for demolition that would maybe never come, gardens overrun with grass that partially hid half-buried skeletal remains of ancient mattresses and other rotting protrudences. The carcass of an old VW Beetle nestled in the only house that had a driveway, the grass was almost level to its roof.

"So why this one? Out of all these other luxury homes."

Tony ignored Danny's question and climbed up over a dirt mound between a crumbling stone wall. Danny followed Tony down the side of the house, kicking rubbish from out of his path as he went. At the back of the house Danny was surprised to see a strong, secure door that was bolted with a chunky combination padlock. "Ha, now we're fucked."

Tony deftly aligned six different numbers, cracked the padlock, opened the heavy door and shoved Danny into darkness.

Danny saw a remarkably well-kept kitchen in the second before Tony secured the door and they were back in black.

"There's a torch, wait," Tony said, a barely perceptible whisper, he fumbled about on a work surface and a beam of light lit a twin ring gas stove, a mug tree and tea and coffee caddies before cutting across grey linoleum towards a closed door. "This way."

Danny tailed obediently behind. "T, what is this place?"

Tony ignored him, left the kitchen and entered what was a small living room. He directed the light at a circular coffee table in the centre which was a graveyard of tealights old and unused. A large box of matches sat amongst the wax-filled foil cups, Tony struck a match and began to light the little candles.

As illumination was slowly brought to the room Danny was surprised to see a red leather three-piece suite that looked expensive, a wooden panelled bar sat in one corner beneath one of the boarded windows. Dotted here and there upon the surfaces of small tables and the corners of a mantlepiece were glasses of various types, some half full, the remnants of a party or some kind of social gathering.

Danny didn't know what to think, none of this could be above board, some kind of doss house where his brother and his mates did whatever it was gay people do. He didn't know his brother anymore; they had grown estranged as adolescence had taken over and having a gay brother had never gone down too well with Neeper and the other members of the GMC. Danny wondered about the aftermath of the massacre and the gang he had been part of, who was even left now?

All that was over and done with, they had been ripped apart with the rest of the town. He tried to push away the memories of his friends being torn down and concentrated on Tony. His older brother was all he had left.

Tony had come to the rescue just like when they were kids, queer or not, he was tougher than any of the gang members. He felt guilty for not knowing anything about his brother other than that he fancied blokes instead of girls and that he had been seeing some weird, lanky dude with a bad perm like someone from an eighties music video. One of the wolves had gotten to him before it killed the Twins. Was he alright? They had been through so much and all Tony had done was be the protective big brother. What about him?

"This place is cool," Danny tried to sound grateful, was grateful. "Is this where you come with your mates?"

Tony's face paled, "Yeah, you could say that." He pointed to the settee and Danny crashed onto it. "Sit here and chill out a bit. Get some sleep or something. I've got to call one of my mates and see if someone will bring us some stuff. Stay here, don't go prying anywhere."

Tony took the torch and left the room, phone in hand.

Chapter 9

A seed of niggling suspicion grew inside Danny. His brother always came across as clean-cut, law-abiding, yet this whole place stunk of corruption.

There was money involved, the furniture and carpets did not look cheap. Danny wondered if Tony was part of something big. That was all he needed.

Slight anger swelled up inside him, if Tony was up to illegal shit it made him the world's largest hypocrite.

He kicked at the arm of the sofa and stared at the door his brother went through. The candles lit the first two steps of a narrow staircase leading up. Beside it another door, he supposed a closet, he saw a heavy sliding bolt and noticed a peculiarity. It had a spyhole. "What the fuck?"

*

"Mr Tepes, it's me," Tony said quietly into the phone.

A dry laugh came from the speaker. "Caller ID, dear boy. I trust you are at the house now?"

Tony nodded, pointlessly, and sat down at the foot of a king-size bed. "Yeah, thanks for letting us stay here."

"Anytime, Tony, anytime." Bartholomew cleared his throat. "So, is this brother of yours as handsome as you are?"

Cold nausea seized Tony. "Don't even think about it! He's not even sixteen."

Bartholomew chuckled. "Like that matters nowadays, just means more money, but rest assured, I only jest," he paused, "but who knows what roads we shall travel down in the future."

"No. No way. I don't want him to know about any of this stuff," Tony snapped before adding, "please."

"Relax, you can trust me, Tony, you know that. We have always had one another's backs, you and I, and whilst I've missed you being around these past few weeks I knew you would be back."

Tony was silent, he hadn't planned on returning, before all this crazy werewolf shit kicked off he was planning on severing all ties and stopping this life he started. Somewhere else, another universe, Tony would take the money he saved and move away, leaving Boxford, the town and its people. Hell, maybe if he had stayed with Christian it wouldn't have even been that bad. At least he had a car, cars meant escape. An image in his head of a towering beast swiping its paw, flensing the skin from his ex-boyfriend's face, the same face he made laugh, cry and mad with anger. Christian knew all about what Tony was getting up to, had known all about the prostitution, it was the main reason why Tony ended things with him. He couldn't afford anyone else finding out. When he ended their relationship Christian even sunk to excruciating cringe-worthy levels and sent numerous text messages begging Tony to let him be one of his customers.

"Are you still there?" Bartholomew purred.

"Yeah, I'm still here. Nowhere else to go," Tony whispered.

"Look, I don't know anything about the situation you're in, Tony, but I'm happy for you to confide in me. A lot of strange things have been happening in Boxford from what I've heard. All complete and utter nonsense no doubt. Or at least certain aspects of it most surely are, but

I'm willing to bet a lot of it has to do with this notorious hoodlum gang from the Green Man Estate. Am I right?"

Tony grunted in confirmation.

"And I'm also willing to bet your brother has something to do with the gang responsible for all this hoo-ha, yes?"

"You could say that."

"Just as I thought. Well, I trust you, Tony, but you know the consequences if any of this comes back on me, don't you?"

"Yeah, yeah I know."

"Good. Stay as long as you need. I'll be around in half an hour with everything you need," Bartholomew said warmly then added, "oh, and Tony?"

"Yes?"

"You're going to have to work for this. Work really hard," he ended the call with a dark chuckle.

Tony flopped back onto the unmade bed. Against the policy the sheets were left unkempt after the last person used them. He put his hands over his face and cried.

*

Danny woke himself up scratching at his arm. His sleeve rode up over the wound where the Scotsman's wolf attacked him. It was a raised purple welt. At the rate it was healing it would barely be visible by morning.

He was going to change into one of those fucking things, that was certain but the important question was when? He thought back, the German, Krauss, and his friends, some of them must have been in control of it, their monsters, some even seemed to be against him, the fat, bald guy in particular. This gave him hope. But

Danny wondered how the hell you could fight such a thing. Was it about willpower, self-restraint?

If so, he was fucked.

One Christmas he spent some of his Christmas money on the biggest tin of chocolates he could find and promised he would make it last until New Year.

He caned the whole tin by 3pm Boxing Day and threw up a glorious-tasting chocolaty gruel over his new Adventure Time duvet set.

If it was the same as the films then he would change at the full moon, and, like most people now, he hadn't got a clue as to when the hell that was either. He couldn't even remember the last time he saw the bloody moon let alone what stage of its lunar cycle it was on.

Actually, he could, he remembered when.

Sat in the ancient bus shelter outside Boxford Village Hall, wispy clouds skated across the sphere in the sky making him think of witches and Halloween.

He was continuing his surveillance on Victor Krauss after finding that stuff in his cellar, after seeing the remains in the black bin bag. Brown skin, Spiderman pyjamas.

One by one the old man's friends showed up at the hall with overnight bags.

They watched them, Danny and Germ, wondering what they were up to. Some kind of indoor camp in the new improved, security-mad village hall, all funded by the mysterious Victor Krauss?

Was this their way of stopping themselves from running rampage?

Danny imagined them all handcuffed together.

Perhaps they were trying to save the world from their wrath after all.

But why the bloody massacre throughout the town? Danny asked himself but he already knew the answer. Because you and the rest of the GMC let them out. You antagonised them, hurt them, made their wolves rise to the surface.

If Neeper and the gang hadn't decided to mug Victor Krauss by the canal would any of this have happened, or would their secret have remained?

If he hadn't gone prying into the old man's house, the old man's cellar, and found those journals, the fridge with the blood samples and silver vials, if he hadn't gone snooping would the deaths be prevented?

Overwhelming guilt suffocated Danny, the horror of the coming shitstorm the infection inside his veins had the potential of bringing about.

Danny made a decision then that he had to find the courage and a way to kill himself before the full moon. Whenever that was.

*

Tony slouched through the lounge, face lit by his phone. Both brothers knew they had both been crying but neither mentioned it. "The guy's here with some stuff. I'm going to get it."

"Want me to help?"

"No," Tony said horrified. "I can manage." He went into the kitchen making sure to close the door.

Danny heard the clack of bolts being undone and the metal door slid across. Then muffled voices.

"I have everything you need," Bartholomew said from beneath the hood of his green raincoat. "And some other things you haven't thought of."

He loitered in the open doorway and handed over some shopping bags.

FERAL

"Never fear, Tony, dear, I'm not coming in anyway. I have a prior engagement today. Let me just run through what I have for you." He lowered his hood and shook back his long hair. "Right, we have two digital watches. You'll be missing your mod-cons and I highly doubt you youngsters wear watches that don't need to be charged with a USB. Two changes of clothing, each. There's a twenty-four-hour launderette not too far from here. You can't stay inside forever. This is just to get you set up. Who knows, maybe one day when I have both Scarborough brothers working for me I may even be able to get you both new identities."

Bartholomew casually pressed his tongue into his cheek to hide his enjoyment of watching Tony squirm. "I know, I know, I'm far too generous." His obsidian eyes bore into Tony's and all traces of his usual camp edge vanished. "I believe in taking care of my possessions."

"How do you know our surname?" Tony stammered.

Bartholomew laughed. "Oh, I've known since I paid a visit to your curly-haired beau, Christian, the other month. Other than that you two boys are this region's most wanted. All. Over. The. News."

Tony felt his legs buckle.

"Relax. The photos they showed were utter bilge. Amazing how we can take spectacular photos of Jupiter and yet the best we can hope for with CCTV is a granular blur." He waved his words away like smoke. "And besides, everyone's all hyped-up over this werewolf malarkey. I can't believe people are buying that poppycock. I've included some hair dye. Probably a good idea to get rid of the Jimmy Savile hairdo, no matter how much the punters love a beautiful blonde. Good job you've still got running water, I say," Bartholomew beamed at the ashen-faced Tony and raised his hood.

"Oh, and speaking of punters, inside one of those bags is a diary with your schedule for the following week. Make sure you're accommodating, there's a good chap."

He made to go but turned back. "If your brother's any trouble just stick him in the cellar, Billy's not back from Thailand for another week."

Danny glared over his brother's shoulder expecting someone to accompany him into the room as he entered with the shopping bags but he came in alone. "Where's your mate?"

Tony was sullen. "Trust me, you don't want to meet him."

He set the bags down and began to rifle through them, laying the items out on the carpet.

Bread, powdered milk, instant noodles, plastic cutlery, biscuits, all supermarket value.

The cheapest money could buy.

Plain clothes; logo-free t-shirts, tracksuits and trainers. No underwear. A power bar, a standard Pay As You Go mobile phone and two digital watches.

Two pots of brown hair dye and a handwritten note of instructions.

Beneath the items was a thick black diary.

"Jesus, it's like being in the nick," Danny said, eyeing the meagre offerings.

"Yep," Tony seriously wondered whether prison would be a safer and better option. He was impressed that Bartholomew chose a dye which was the same shade as his natural hair colour.

Vanity was something he was going to have to put on hold for the foreseeable future.

FERAL

With their matching tracksuits and natural coloured hair the two boys were going to look like brothers again for the first time since they were little.

There was some dude in the Bible whose power was all in his hair. Tony hoped to Christ changing his appearance wouldn't destroy his confidence that much.

"I better go and get rid of this bleached mess if we want to go out again," Tony said, pulling at his hair as though he hated it.

Danny doubted it would make a difference, there was no mistaking his brother, plus he had been every hair colour under the sun anyway.

"How long do we have to stay here?"

Tony shrugged. "I don't know. Hopefully not long. My friend, he can get us new identities if we need them."

Danny's eyes went wild.

His brother showed more layers to his involvement in the crime world. "Jesus."

"I know, I know. I'm hoping it won't come to that. I just wish we knew what was going on out there."

"It's not that." Danny said, trying to contain the anger in his voice, "it's all this." He waved his hands around the room. "You've spent so much time in the past trying to get me to stay away from the GMC and all the time you're mixed up with people that have secret fucking houses, can get secret identification and fuck knows what else? What is this place, huh? Do they run drugs from here, or what?"

"What this place is, or isn't, is irrelevant right now," Tony said, matching his brother's anger. "We have nowhere else. Yeah I'm a hypocrite, okay? But just because I do wrong things doesn't mean I want my little brother doing the same and potentially ruining his life too."

"Yeah, well I've done that anyway haven't I?"

"What's done is done. This is where we are. Now change out of those things. I'm going to dye my hair and then we'll get something to eat."

FERAL

Chapter 10

Bartholomew sweated under the weight of Lee. The boy was heavier than he looked and since his mini-stroke five years ago his strength had never really returned to its former glory.

He bound the washing line around the bathroom door handle once more, he had absolute faith that it would hold, it had done so before, and surveyed his handy work. It didn't take long to set up this little device but he had always been good at jobs around the house. The shower curtain rail was reinforced, it could hold three hundred pounds, the shower tray was half a foot wider than necessary, not really noticeable unless highlighted. Now he was pushing sixty it was the lifting that got to him. He knew he could rig some sort of pulley system up but that would to be as inconspicuous as the rest of the set-up.

Subduing the boy wasn't hard. Most youngsters, most people, had a weakness, a vice, whether it be for alcohol, sex or illicit substances. Bartholomew could provide all three, if necessary.

Lee got intoxicated very fast, desperate to show Bartholomew gratitude for accepting him to become his new fledgling vampire. Lee drunkenly slobbered on him for what felt like an eternity before the sedatives took effect and he passed out across Bartholomew's thighs. And now he hung upside-down, wrists and ankles bound together, above Bartholomew's shower tray.

Bartholomew took five to massage the muscles in his neck and shoulders and watched as Lee's hair trailed over the plughole. Jesus, he thought, it takes even longer to get going after you've strung them up nowadays, everyone gets harder. Cursing his own mortality he pushed himself off the shower room floor and dragged a large tin bucket from below the sink. He lifted it into the shower tray with a clatter, hugged Lee's head and shoulders and positioned the bucket below.

    Once placed, Bartholomew took an incredibly sharp paring knife and nicked Lee's jugular vein, and sat back with a heavy sigh. The loud hiss of blood against the metal bucket was music to his ears, but the shriek when Lee's eyes sprang open wasn't.

    That wasn't supposed to happen.

    His rapid jerks caused his body to swing around sending thick arterial spray across Bartholomew's chest as he got him in an upside-down bear hug, holding him until he bled out more. A thick gout of blood caught him full in the eyes temporarily blinding him, he panicked and tried to find his feet and Lee's forehead connected with his nose. His head ricocheted off the doorpost, the reinforced shower rail snapped free from the fittings and Lee toppled onto Bartholomew knocking over the blood in the bucket. The remaining life-fluid trickled out of his still-twitching corpse and mingled with the vampire's.

    He hurt, hurt so bad.

    A crust of dried blood covered his face and he was freezing; and felt old, so very old.

    The body of the goth boy had fallen on top of him, a tangle of limbs.

    Bartholomew scrubbed blood from his face with his sleeve, wincing when he touched his nose, hoping to Christ it wasn't broken. He cried out at the egg-shaped lump on his head where he struck the door post.

    As he cleaned the gore from his face he noticed the extent of the damage and yet another injury he hadn't seen.

Not only did Lee pull the bloody shower rail down but the fucking thing nearly skewered him in the process.

He fingered the hole in the centre of his top, there was a tender place on his breastbone. Despite the immense pain and the considerable cock-up, Bartholomew laughed at the irony. An aging vampire nearly impaling himself, having to use a knife instead of his teeth since that was all just a thing of mythology and folklore, feeling like a victim himself and not a fucking drop of blood to make it worth the effort. The dry laughter soon turned to self-pitying sighs as he bemoaned his lot. Things were getting hard, this took weeks to arrange. He hadn't the time, energy or resources he had when he was younger and more prolific.

Blood was the life, that was the problem; and he wasn't getting any.

Bartholomew wasn't what most people would consider a vampire. There were no powers of a supernatural nature, he could not metamorphosise into creeping mists, shapeshift into wolves or bats.

He wasn't a creature of the night.

Sunlight had no effect on him and as he was of Romany ancestry his skin tanned rather than burned, which was great in his younger years.

He believed consumption of the blood and flesh of another person empowered him.

Legend tells that if you consume another's flesh or blood you gain their strength.

He believed it.

Bartholomew hated the word killer, even though that was technically what he was, he had killed dozens of times, but he preferred to think himself a hunter as he used every last piece of his victims.

FERAL

Since he was twenty-three he had, on average, killed one person a year.

He consumed as much of them as possible and destroyed the rest. There were endless ways to dispose of crumbled remains if inventive enough; and he had more than enough tools in his workshop to render their remains to nothing much more than ash.

The important thing was blood, fresh warm blood and to drink it as fresh and as much as possible.

Then he would chill the rest and consume nothing else until it went.

The meat he stripped from the corpses he treated in various different ways, the same with their organs.

Bone marrow was a good stock.

He peered solemnly into the bucket and the sticky lake on the floor. This was the first time he failed.

He hung his head, cursed his bad luck and his own mortality.

He longed for the days when he had blazing sex with multiple consensual partners, sometimes the more adventurous ones were into blood-letting. That was a quick fix between victims and it may have even sufficed if frequent enough but those types of people were too hard to come by. Stalking and killing became the only way, but now he was old and unfit, he couldn't even do that properly.

Bartholomew growled in frustration and kicked out at Lee's body, pushed it off and readied himself to prepare the meat.

Sweat poured as he dragged the corpse through the hall. The boy was a lot heavier than he appeared. He cursed himself for not laminating the floors like he planned many a time before. The thick-pile carpet would be a treat for the forensic team if ever he came under their radar with the amount of people he had brought across its gaudy pattern. No amount of scrubbing would remove everything and lately he didn't seem to care; whether it be the myth that all serial killers desired their own capture, or whether he thought himself untouchable or just lucky. A lancing pain shot through the centre of his head and he dropped the body to the floor.

"Oh fuck, oh fuck, oh fuck, oh fuck!"

The feeling passed as soon as it came, he regulated his breathing and proceeded with the original task.

He dragged the corpse under the armpits and stared into the dead man's eyes and saw his own haggard face. He looked scared.

The pain in his head returned, worse, and he toppled forwards on top of the dead boy.

"Oh furrr," he said, his left eye widened in horror when he realised only half of his face worked.

Lying prone on top of the man he just killed, Bartholomew discovered paralysis down the entire right side of his body. Panic grew at an alarming speed and used his left hand and elbow to push the body off him. He reached for his mobile phone in his trousers pocket but the stickiness of the situation reared its head and cackled.

Drool ran freely from the drooping corner of the right side of his mouth. "Oh furrr." He could taste the familiar, but dull, lifeless flavour of his own blood, he had bitten his tongue too. "Oh furrr."

The plastic of the mobile phone pressed against his working hand. Bartholomew weighed up his options and the memory of his first taste of another's blood came with crystal clarity.

Chapter 11

Bartholomew Tepes hadn't been his name then, but his birth name didn't suit the personality he had grown into as a young man, when he finally admitted to himself who — and what— he was.

His first taste of another's blood was long before the birth of Bartholomew Tepes, way back when he was a child.

She was small, freckle-faced, her hair scraped into a brown explosion which raised her eyebrows in surprise.

Kelly Smalley was an appropriate name for a girl of six who didn't look a day over four.

They'd walked home from school together along the path that wound through Goswell's Wood.

Their parents, always the mothers, followed behind as they raced through the trees chasing make-believe imps and fairies.

The Old Hump, a name they'd bestowed, was a half-buried tree root which cut across the footpath, thick and worn smooth by years of footfall, like the coil of a monstrous anaconda that was swimming through the ground.

The Old Hump.

The kids firmly believed it to be a partially buried dinosaur, part of a brontosaurus neck.

Whatever it was, on the day the boy who would grow up to be Bartholomew Tepes first tasted someone else's blood, Kelly Smalley didn't see it, and as her shiny school shoe caught on it during a fairy princess's heroic deed—rescuing cheeky imps from terrifying goblins— she tripped and flew for real.

Her young playmate made haste to her rescue, even though he knew that if his friend was really hurt, it would be a job for the adults.

Kelly lay flat on her face, her red-and-white gingham dress ridden up around her back, exposing her pants. It was the first time he had seen a girl's pants; he preferred his own, they had boats on them. She didn't cry as he'd expected, as he usually did when he tumbled, just lay on her belly, all still.

"Kelly?" he shouted and touched her bare calf with the toe of his brown shoe. "Are you deaded?"

Kelly shook her head, her ponytail flicking from side to side, then sat up and saw the cut splitting the delicate pink pad of her fingertip. She screamed at the sight of her own blood and the cut was very deep, so it was bleeding a lot.

Her young friend, not her boyfriend, heard the frantic caterwauls of their mothers far off, crashing along the overgrown footpath towards them, no doubt imagining every worst-case scenario.

But the boy's initial reaction was to follow his instinct, and his instinct told him to do what he did whenever he'd cut himself.

He squatted down beside her, his jet-black hair dangling over his face, making Kelly think of the little boy in The Jungle Book, and sucked her bleeding digit.

The coppery tang overwhelmed him and even though Kelly naturally pulled away from the strange thing her friend was doing, he held onto her forearm with both hands, eyes screwed shut, as a new and glorious sensation overpowered him.

He sucked and sucked at that finger, and time seemed to freeze him in a world of dark red and black punctuated by the perpetual ringing of Kelly's forever frozen scream.

He felt the blood meet his own, saw it mingle in his veins and felt her essence, her sweetness, her fairy-dust inside him.

Millennia passed in the first consumption of that fluid; he aged, died and was reborn billions of times and he knew, felt, and *was* everything.

And then he was being dragged off his wailing friend, the two mothers shrieking at one another.

"Your ruddy son's bitten her, what the bloody hell is wrong with him?"

A hard slap across the cheek saw off the remaining tingles of euphoria and his mother glared at him with unfamiliar eyes.

He hadn't been allowed to play with Kelly Smalley afterwards, despite having mumbled his garbled version of events.

He was labelled the school weirdo, and so began the slow descent into the solitary hermitude that adulthood would bring.

*

Bartholomew came round from the half-dazed dream about his childhood; the artificial light coming into the hallway through the lounge told him a considerable length of time had passed.

It was late, and he couldn't feel anything on the right side of his body.

With his one working hand, he swept the carpet for his mobile phone and found it lying in a damp patch.

He mentally prayed that it wasn't ruined.

The phone worked, thank God, but his right eye didn't.

Only ten percent of battery life left.

With a trembling thumb, he swiped open the screen, found the boy's number on the phone, and typed.

COME. NOW. BREAK DOOR DOWN.

His arm slumped to the carpet, the phone still clutched tightly.

The boy would come. He always did as he was told and was not one for questioning things. Needed the money, too.

As he waited for his dutiful servant to arrive, he drove away the mounting panic by bringing to mind the first time he and the boy had met. Focusing his thoughts reassured him that there didn't seem to be any mental damage; well, none that wasn't already there.

Chapter 12

Boxford was a cesspit.

Numerous regeneration projects had aimed to sift away some of the detritus from its bursting seams, but most had failed within a couple of decades.

The latest project, The Green Man Estate, erected in the seventies, boasted modern, environmentally-friendly living, consisting of five high-rise tower blocks.

Slowly, over the years, it had degraded from what was once a close-knit community into a hotbed of drugs and crime, with most of the local youth aspiring to be part of the Green Man Crew.

But mugging, addictions, and random acts of cruelty weren't the only things lurking beneath the greasy surface of Boxford's waters; prostitution was another.

At a young age, Bartholomew had discovered the levels of depravity some men would stoop to, and the things they would do if they thought themselves beyond capture.

He was fourteen when he lost his virginity—unwillingly—to a friend of his father's.

The drunken layabout had always looked at him funny, and would make snide comments about his long, 'girlish' hair and his tendency to stay quiet. Then one day, after a family gathering he'd been forced into at the old Boxford village hall, the man forced him into a piss-stinking toilet cubicle, thrust his head against the spiderwebbed porcelain, and he had no say in the matter.

Afterwards, the family friend, his father's acquaintance, emerged dazed, as though what he'd done had been beyond his control. A compulsion he couldn't ignore.

Bartholomew left the stinking lavatories with his trousers and underwear down, walked into a room filled with cousins, uncles, and aunties, and shrieked louder than the cheesy seventies music blaring from the speakers.

No one quite knew what exactly occurred when Bartholomew's father stormed into the toilets after taking one look at his son, but a few months later he was convicted for the murder of his friend.

The man was found, his neck snapped. All his father said on the matter was, "He got what he deserved."

Three weeks after settling on the E-Wing of Sudbury Prison, Bartholomew's father was found in his cell, hanging by his bedsheets.

His mother, estranged from him yet still officially his guardian, blamed the loss entirely on her son. She accused him of having flirty, girlish ways, and said he had been asking for it.

Blatant fabrications.

From a young age, there seemed to be a piece missing from the jigsaw of Bartholomew's mind.

He never did feel mental anguish, emotional pain, for anyone other than himself, even when his father hanged himself in jail. His mother was merely a provider of food, shelter and money, although the latter was very sparse. She routinely displayed her hatred for him in every way possible.

Throughout his youth, his obsession with the macabre grew, from reading about fairy-tale monstrosities to researching the myths and legends that had inspired them.

After his encounter with Kelly Smalley's blood, he had become drawn to the most famous of horror archetypes- the vampire.

He dove headfirst into everything vampirical he could beg, borrow, or steal.

Dracula was read routinely, picked apart, and studied like a manual, but he ridiculed the supernatural being.

The legendary figure Vlad the Impaler came under his radar; he was in awe of the fifteenth-century Romanian sadist.

The detailed descriptions of his alleged deeds set Bartholomew's teenage libido a-quiver and ignited something he knew had lain dormant: his bloodlust.

Unlike most people who grew up to be emotionless serial killers, Bartholomew didn't have a history of animal abuse; nothing on which to practise and hone his craft, so he studied the theory of murder, vivisection and torture, although the act he found the most intriguing was the consumption of another's blood.

Sometimes he would use the blade of his Swiss army knife, the last gift from his father, to cut lines into the taut flesh of his forearms; only an inch or so, enough to take a drink.

It didn't matter how many times he self-harmed, even when he drank enough to make him bring back his dinner, nothing compared to the taste of Kelly Smalley's blood that day in Goswell's Wood.

Bartholomew had been nineteen when he committed his first murder. Luck, or fate, played a part in finally taking his killing virginity.

FERAL

His mother was a haemophiliac; her blood had no clotting ability. This meant that when she bled, she would bleed and bleed and bleed.

They had ignored each other consistently since his father's death. His mother continued to run the books of her husband's building firm but handed over the labour side of things to their son. Bartholomew had promised his father he would continue the family business. Despite loathing the work, he became an accomplished craftsman.

Neither mother nor son cared about their living arrangements; each served their purpose. The son did the physical jobs his mother could not manage, and the mother made sure there was always food to eat and clean clothes to wear.

He was permitted a small allowance, paid weekly, from wages he never saw, to do with as he wished, and this was mostly squirrelled away or spent on ludicrously priced specialist books and magazines. Books and magazines on bondage, blood-letting, and sadomasochism.

But none of these things ever ventured down the dark avenues he really wanted to pry into.

The fateful day came in the July after his nineteenth birthday. Friday was fish-and-chips day, a tradition his father had started and which his mother had continued since his passing. Sometimes she would still buy a disgusting patty of battered roe, which his father used to favour, and she would mulch the brown sludge into a thick paste against her gums whilst tears ran freely down her face.

That particular Friday, after a long, hard day erecting a giant conservatory, the first thing he saw when he came in through the back door was a pile of chips on the kitchen floor.

The second thing he saw was blood, a great big pool of it, spreading on the floor beneath the fallen meal.

His mother sat pale-faced but relieved that her son had finally come home. A tea towel was pressed firmly to her leg. "Don't just stand there, ring a bloody ambulance, for God's sake!"

Bartholomew, without hesitation, stepped into the kitchen, closed the door, locked it behind him, and smiled coldly. "Oh dear, what have you done to yourself?"

Fear brought a speck of colour back into his mother's alabaster cheeks. "Help me, son, please."

He squatted, his work boots making prints in the pool gathering on the tiles. "Let. Me. See."

"No, son," she said, a kindness; a weakness, even, in her voice for the first time since he was a child.

She tried her best to hold the blood-sodden cloth against her leg but he grabbed her bony wrist and yanked it away.

She was the child now.

A thick, glorious ribbon of ruby spurted from a gash on her thigh and splattered onto his chin. Three droplets landed on his lower lip. His tongue flicked out instinctively; the zing of his mother's blood fired his taste buds and he — quite literally — saw red.

Bloodlust took over and he used his lithe nineteen-year-old labourer's strength to clasp his mother's wrists in one hand whilst pushing her legs wide open with the other.

She gave out a baffled, sickened whimper as her son latched onto her skin with the same vigour and enthusiasm he'd had as a baby, this time sucking at a different kind of life-fluid, pumping copiously from her femoral artery, his fingers kneading at the doughy flesh of her thighs as they once had her breasts.

He made such a glutton of himself he passed out at the end of his frenzy.

He came round on his side in a sea of congealing blood mingled with his own vomit, his mother slumped against the stove, white-faced and glassy-eyed. Thick purple fingerprints were bruised into the soft flesh around the wound where he had held onto her, making it look as though he had tried to pinch the cut closed, willing it to heal.

He wondered what the hell she had cut herself on and then saw a knife lying amidst the chips; she'd always made her own.

Slowly, not too sure of his stability, he got to his feet and caught his reflection in a small mirror hanging on the wall. It had been salvaged from a barber's his father frequented.

The mirrored glass was an etching of a Victorian barbershop beneath a brace of crossed cutthroat razors and the name 'Bartholomew Bros.'

He saw his reflection: jet-black hair, dark, impenetrable eyes, pale skin, everything below his cheeks stained red with his mother's blood.

He hissed like something feline; real vampires had reflections then, fancy that.

His teeth felt stronger, sharper, capable of ripping apart raw meat, capable of piercing the cartilage between the bones.

He felt that within his mother's death he had *become*, been reborn, a baptism in blood.

He was now like Vladimir Tepes.

It was a monumental turning point: he would become something now, something powerful, all-knowing.

He caught the barbershop logo again, and one last time he smiled his wicked red grin and knew what he would call himself.

Afterwards he sorted the complications of his mother's death. The cause, blood loss. His reason for not calling for help sooner, a squeamish reaction to seeing his mother in a pool of her own blood, causing him to vomit and black out.

It affected his notoriety for being the town weirdo.

People saw him as someone more human then, albeit one with a weak stomach, but he was increasingly mocked for letting his mother die.

It did no harm to his reputation, though, and now he had discovered his goal in life, it would be appropriate for people to think him puny and pathetic.

His mother had left no will, and as he was the only surviving relative, everything went to him. It was strange to have access to a side of his parents' life he had not known before, and he was surprised by what riches they had been hoarding.

At twenty years old, he was in charge of a large building firm and had the accumulated profits of a forty-year-old business at his disposal, but as before, he spent very little.

He took on the managerial role of the firm, keeping his old name for the day job, whilst he set up everything he needed for his alter ego, Bartholomew Tepes.

Since his mother's death, all he could think about was other people's blood. Of course, he understood the risks involved in its consumption.

As he delved into specialist books and magazines, his confidence grew with the new, darkly gothic visage he had created.

His contacts began to widen and he found out where other wannabe vampires hung out.

Dark, sordid, cellar nightclubs that played slow, industrial music, where everyone moved in sluggish, drugged movements.

Illegal substances were actively taken, carnal desires acted upon, but although many of these people claimed they were real vampires, rarely did he meet anyone who would willingly let him drink their blood, or if he did, he would usually cause great offence by wanting, or trying, to take too much.

He found an intense rush only ever came if the blood were imbibed straight from the vein.

He would discover that at a later date.

That came during one of his greedy times. A buxom woman had been lured back to his domain by his new-found charm and good looks.

They had sex, something he cared little for but which he could perform well enough for others' satisfaction when required. In this instance, it was the lady's condition for the blood-letting. She turned her nose up at his clean Stanley knife and tossed it to the floor beside the bed and produced a lavish silver dagger with a ruby encrusted handle.

Bartholomew saw it was a cheap replica of something typically gothic, an ornamental letter-opener, nothing more, its top was the only part sharp enough to pierce skin. She used it to nick the flesh on his pectorals, barely a cat scratch, and moaned and quivered with pleasure as she licked away the droplets.

This went on for several minutes, several tedious minutes, whilst she ground and gyrated beneath him, trying to rouse him into another bout of sexual gratification.

This wasn't what he wanted.

He wanted this woman—he knew that as he stared at her pale flesh and the blue networks criss-crossing her perfect skin—but for other purposes.

In one smooth, spontaneous movement, he swung his arm down, picked up the Stanley knife, pushed a segment of blade out with his thumb and swiped it across her jugular. "My turn," he said, smiling at her blissful expression of shock as he showed her the bloody blade.

He pressed her arms to the bed before they had a chance to flail, and his lips against that pretty crimson slash on her neck.

At some point, before the intense rush of hot blood was all he knew, he felt himself become erect and enter her.

The aftermath of this kill was messy; a lot of blood went to waste. Next time would be better if preparations were made, not just for the murder, but for the collection and storage of the remaining fluids.

It wasn't until his second victim that he tried cannibalism and discovered a more economical—as he liked to think of it—means of disposal.

She, his first aside from his mother, was unplanned and it had taken a lot to clean up afterwards.

A very deep grave in a very remote field one night took care of her charred remains, but her disposal haunted him the older he got. He was certain she would be the one who would get him caught.

His third victim was the first step down a path to a prosperous new career change.

The building firm was profitable, but times were forever changing, money could get him what he wanted more and more.

For the right amount of cash, there was a certain class of prostitute who would let him use sterile equipment to extract a pint of blood.

It didn't have the same kick as cutting, and he wasn't successful with the alternative dentistry avenues he investigated, but it served a purpose between victims. As ever, though, greed got the better of him.

He took too much from one prostitute, and she blacked out—whereupon he took the rest.

He was in the process of hanging her body over his bathtub to drain when a man beat the front door in and caught him, quite literally, red-handed.

Luckily for him, he didn't hesitate, and stabbed the man as soon as he laid eyes on him.

When he searched his mobile phone, he found out the man had been the woman's pimp.

He hadn't seen a mobile phone before. It was like a small walkie-talkie; they were the latest fad.

Using his funds and his skills at violence and manipulation, Bartholomew gradually poached the dead pimp's workers, and twenty years later, with the building firm long since sold, he lived off the riches of his one and only trade.

That was how he ended up meeting the boy who would save his life as he lay in a semi-comatose state on the hallway floor beneath the body of his latest victim, after having a massive stroke.

A message alert interrupted the fractured life story that was passing before his eyes.

The movements in his only working arm were difficult, he was exhausted.

He thumbed open the message, it was the boy.

Bartholomew felt a familiar rage as the boy's usual excuse came into play but he had no choice other than to rest his head and wait.

He had no more strength.

His hand dropped.

The phone's message screen filled the hall with blue illumination.

BE THERE IN 5. JUST NEED TO SORT MY BRO OUT. TONY

FERAL

Chapter 13
1945

In the days following his escape, Victor wandered the countryside, his attention turned inward. He focused on the changes within, on new feelings and emotions. The influence of something *other*, and the remarkable feats of endurance and strength for someone of his age.

Schäfer, the father, had advised him that to beat one's wolf, one must prove more selfish, more stubborn than it.

Victor took and he took from these new gifts the alien beast inside offered but gave nothing back.

At night, he camped in the Black Forest, keeping a close watch on the moon, knowing that when it was full, it would be time to face his toughest trial.

He hoped to find Gwen long before that happened.

Gwen's condition meant she spent a lot of time reliving the past, and as it was Victor's nature to analyse and study, he pinpointed the era into which she flitted back and forth.

Somewhere between the ages of five and thirty.

He deduced that given the sudden abilities he had, she would do one of two things, and each involved the same outcome. She would search for him, possibly a younger version of him, and go back home to the village where she had grown up, where they had lived after marrying. At his present rate of travel, he should arrive at the village the next day. He hoped there would be time to find somewhere secure before the full moon.

Victor saw the devastation when he left the canopy of trees and descended into the valley. Their little village by the Rhine had changed from a vision of picturesque tranquillity to a black rash of wasteland.

Only remnants of roads remained.

Something, a bomb, no doubt, had destroyed the church. Fires spread throughout the buildings, consuming everything. Smoke still curled from blackened roof beams.

The survivors would have gone to the next town ten miles away.

Would they have taken Gwen with them?

There was no time to search. The full moon would rise soon and he needed to find shelter and fight his transformation.

Searching through the debris of the fallen village was fruitless: there were no signs of life, no answers.

He made his way along the riverbank, each step leaving him more depleted.

A heavy weight lay on his shoulders, an inner darkness clouded his mind, defeat washed over him black and thick. His legs gave way and he fell painfully to the ground, his new vitality gone.

The knots of his joints ripened — he could hear them creaking — as the pain of old age hit him and left him defeated.

Memories of Gwen swamped him.

Maybe it had all been for nothing.

What if she is dead?

It would be better if she was.

The Rhine's current carried the water past his line of vision in a gentle silver swathe, and he wondered how easy it would be to walk into its flow.

Just walk.

The water was so inviting, sparkling in the sun, he remembered his youth, when he used to swim in the waters.

"Ha!" Victor gave a hollow laugh, more to prove he had control over his voice than anything else. "No such luck, Wolf!"

He braced himself against the pain in his knees and forced himself to his feet. "I will not quit until I find my wife."

The going was slow; he cleared the village and began to climb the other side of the valley. As afternoon turned to dusk he found his new abilities returning, his senses becoming stronger. He knew these were signs of the imminent transformation.

Within the next few hours the wolf inside him would try to make its first appearance, and if he wanted to be in control, be the animal's master, he needed to resist that change, stop the metamorphosis.

This, according to the Schäfers, was the first and hardest step. All he could think of was the father's incredulous, laughing face as he told him of his experience of resisting the first transformation.

"The wolf will try to destroy you, both body and mind."

The forest was alive with scents that overpowered his heightened senses; most were familiar, but some were not.

He smelled something metallic and headed towards it automatically.

There was no plan other than to tackle the full force of the transformation wherever he stood. When the light faltered, he could still see, and found the source of the metal.

A shelter covering someone's woodpile.

Logs, stacked beneath a corrugated iron roof, barely high enough for him to stand below; but he was grateful for its shelter as he knew by the rising of his temperature and the glittering of the moon between the trees that his wolf was coming.

Chapter 14

Juliet wanted the nurse to hurry up, walk faster, she would have raced on ahead if she'd known which direction to take.

There wasn't far to go to the ITU but the corridor was busy with staff and patients. An orderly blocked the entrance to the ward with a stretcher, on it a middle-aged man with scraggly grey-black hair.

Juliet saw his horrid lopsided face and averted her eyes.

Better to die than to live like that.

They followed the patient onto the ward.

The nurse turned the opposite way and led her to a section where they had made a meagre attempt at making it child-friendly, with colourful murals on the wall.

Her children were in a room on their own; she burst into tears as soon as she lay eyes on them. A chorus of "Mummy" came from the two heads poking out of the sheets. Wires and clips connected them to numerous machines.

Juliet fell to her knees between the beds, put a hand on each of them, and thanked God they were still alive.

"I'll give you a few minutes and then the doctor would like to see you, if that's okay?" the young nurse said, gently resting a hand on her shoulder.

Juliet nodded and gazed in gratitude at her children's snotty faces.

Juliet thought it was nice to see a woman doctor for a change, although she was younger than she had expected, and insisted the children and Juliet called her 'Doctor Charlotte.'

Kayleigh struck up an instant rapport with her, instantly falling in awe and making her day by telling her she looked like Disney's Princess Jasmine. Kiran was at an age where he either showed off or went suspiciously quiet around beautiful young ladies; fortunately for Juliet and Doctor Charlotte, he had chosen the latter this time.

Juliet even found herself smitten by the woman and threw compliments at her without seeming to have any control over her words. "Oh, I love your hair… You can't be a doctor, you're too young."

"I'm almost thirty-two, I'll have you know," Doctor Charlotte said with a coy smile.

"That's *really* old," Kiran said, emerging from his shell. "But not as old as you, Mummy."

"Shut up, dummy. Doctor Charlotte isn't old at all," Kayleigh said, propping herself up on an elbow.

"Like chalk and cheese, these two," said Juliet.

"Yes," Kayleigh said, "I'm chalk because I create beautiful art and Kiran is cheese because he smells of feet."

Doctor Charlotte laughed hard and perched on Kayleigh's bed and looked at both kids. "I'm going to have to keep a close eye on you two, aren't I?"

The children tried their best to look as innocent as possible.

"Now, if I promise to come back after dinner and say goodnight, would you mind if I took your mummy outside in the corridor for five minutes?"

"Will you bring me one of those face masks the surgeons wear when they cut people up?" Kiran asked; clearly this would be the deciding factor for him.

Doctor Charlotte grinned. "I'll bring you gloves, *and* a hat, if I'm longer than five minutes. Do we have a deal?"

"And a ste-," —Kayleigh struggled with the word, and glanced at her brother, who nodded encouragement —"stethoscope?"

"No. But I'll let you have a go with mine."

Something unspoken passed between the two children and they nodded in unison.

Out in the corridor, Doctor Charlotte had a wide smile. "They're adorable."

"But are they going to be okay?" Juliet said, lowering her tone.

"It's early days. I can't say there's not going to be any mental trauma, we still don't really know what has happened and there are one or two inconsistencies that need addressing. But physically, at the moment, they are fine." The doctor stifled a giggle at what she was about to say. "In fact, Kiran is better than fine."

"Why? What do you mean, better than fine?"

"Obviously, we have his medical records here at the hospital, but can you confirm that he had his appendix removed when he was two?"

Juliet nodded. Her dad had been a godsend then, looking after Kayleigh even when she cried all night for her brother. "Yes, he did, right here in this hospital. Why, what's wrong?"

Doctor Charlotte uttered that same disbelieving laugh. "Well, nothing is *wrong*. It's just that his appendix scar is one of the inconsistencies."

"Why, what's the matter with it? Did it reopen? Is it infected? What?"

"No, Juliet. Nothing like that, nothing bad." Doctor Charlotte couldn't even meet her gaze as she told her. "It's just ...the scar. Well, it's vanished."

"How the bloody hell—" Juliet began, but the doctor, now free of her burden, cut her off.

"That's not the only thing. The blood on the children's pyjamas was their own, yet they had no visible injuries and neither of them can remember what happened. They were asking for you, and their grandad."

Light-headed, Juliet slid down against the wall.

Doctor Charlotte helped her to a nearby chair.

"I'm okay, I'm okay," she insisted.

Doctor Charlotte sat beside her. "Juliet, I don't know what's going on with your children, or how this happened, but I promise that I will do my best to find out. But the important thing is, here and now, they are okay."

Juliet nodded and forced a smile.

As the doctor left, she thought about the woman in the ambulance outside the tower block; the worker from the café. She'd asked her what the hell had happened then, why the building was surrounded by police and ambulances.

"Them things on the fucking telly, that's what. Fucking werewolves."

Her knowledge of the supernatural was limited; she hated all that scary stuff. All she knew was that they changed at full moon, didn't like silver, and the kicker: they weren't bloody real.

A memory resurfaced: the kids watching some old cartoon, Scooby Doo. There was a werewolf in it, which had its tail chopped off, and it had grown back.

They could do that sort of thing, too, apparently.

But that was a cartoon — they weren't real.

Even though there were stories about them in the newspapers and they were one of the most recognised horror monsters out there, *they weren't real.*

Even though her children had been found in remnants of their own clothing, covered in pints of their own blood, and were somehow alive and unscathed in the middle of a massacre, *werewolves weren't real.*

She remembered her dad's newfound lease of life and energy, how she suspected he'd been taking something dodgy from one of his dealer friends, more than just the odd sniff of weed, which he'd sworn he had quit.

So much death, so many witnesses, even though a newspaper was trying to pin it all on the Green Man Crew.

"Oh Jesus, Dad, what the hell have you done to my babies?"

FERAL

Chapter 15

A hammering on the door brought him out of a short bout of unconsciousness.

Everything on his left side hurt; pain was preferable to the sheer non-existence of feeling on the right.

The letterbox rattled.

"Hello, Mr Tepes."

It was the boy.

He had told him to break down the door.

Bartholomew tried to call out, but it felt as though his lips were sewn shut.

He slapped his hand against the floor and reached for his phone.

BREKFUCKINDORDWN.

Just swiping his thumb across the screen used up what little energy he had left.

If the idiot didn't do as he was told, Tepes was fucked.

He heard the boy's phone and heard him finally kicking against the lock.

Tony didn't have a clue how to break a front door in. Kicking at the lock felt as though it would dislocate his knee.

Something was wrong with Tepes, that was obvious, but Tony had witnessed enough carnage to be prepared for whatever state he was in.

The door was solid.

He backed up the small path and slammed his shoulder into the wood and instantly fell on his arse.

He wasn't built for this; he was skinny, too light.

FERAL

The house was a simple detached affair.

He scanned the upstairs and downstairs windows, hoping one had been left open, but the house was completely secure.

There was no way in.

The only thing he could do was phone an ambulance, anonymously, and do another runner. But if he did, Bartholomew would string him up for absconding.

He rang Bartholomew's mobile, not knowing if he was in a fit state to answer.

The phone rang and rang. He was about to give up but Tepes answered it and barked incomprehensible gibberish down the line. He sounded heavily sedated, or drunk.

Tony knew basic first aid and recognised slurred speech as a sign of something serious. "I can't get in. I'm going to call an ambulance, but I can't stick around. I'm sorry, I'm in trouble."

More babble. Bartholomew sounded livid, on the verge of total breakdown, Tony thought. But he was convinced he had heard the word *shed*.

The phone cut out mid-call.

Tony had an idea. The shed would have the tools he would need to get the door open.

A small shed at the rear of the house was a treasure trove, heavily stocked with all kinds of tools, kept in pristine condition. Tony selected a long crowbar, so heavy it took both hands to lift it. He attacked the less than sturdy back door with the iron bar and marvelled at how easily it came open.

He called out as he entered the-sized kitchen.

Bartholomew lay in the hallway outside the bathroom, the body of a young man lying beside him, his throat slit.

A hiss of what Tony presumed was bitter laughter came from Bartholomew as he focused his one good eye on him.

*

Tony didn't need the information from the first aid course at the supermarket café to know Bartholomew had suffered a stroke; the signs were obvious.

Although he had witnessed more than his fair share of brutality over the last few days, and knew Bartholomew was a less than savoury character, his initial assumption was that a sex game had gone horribly wrong. However, as he rushed to his lifeline's aid, the only one he could turn to for money and protection, he saw the cord and the bucket.

This was a premeditated murder, no doubt about it. Tony felt his gorge rise as he took in the dead man and the lake of blood that covered the bathroom floor.

There were darker depths to the fathoms of Bartholomew Tepes.

A moment's hesitation was all it took for the murderer to raise his only working hand and feebly show a message typed on the screen, ready to send to the police.

Brief and to the point, it named the location of the Scarborough brothers' current hideout.

Tony breathed deeply to quell the urge to vomit and felt a tugging at his trousers.

Tepes pointed weakly towards a door to his left.

Tony's hand shook as he pulled the door handle down.

A cupboard full of cleaning materials.

Tepes smiled crookedly and moved his head just a fraction of a nod.

Tony swallowed his rising bile and reached for the mop and bucket.

He knew he had to be quick; with a stroke, time was of the essence. But he needed to clean up Tepes' mess first.

After he had tackled the seemingly endless task of mopping up the blood, he double-bagged the mop and bucket in a pair of black bin bags.

Disposing of the corpse and getting Bartholomew medical attention was paramount.

Flashbacks from the night in the park still sickened him: how he and Danny had helped the old bald man pile up the slaughtered victims before setting fire to them.

"Should I burn it?" Tony said, a thought out loud, not really a question he expected Tepes to be capable of answering.

But Tepes did answer. "No. Free-er. Sed. Gar-en."

Tony stared at his sudden animated face and tried to decipher what he was trying to tell him.

Something about the garden?

"No, I can't bury him, it'll take too long. You need to get to the hospital."

"No!" Bartholomew shouted, spittle flying and his hand slapping at the floor. "Free-er. In. Gar-en sed."

"Freezer?" Tony knew he was right as soon as he'd said it, and figured out what was expected of him not long after.

There wasn't anywhere to bury the body in Bartholomew's garden; it was completely concreted over. Thankfully, it was also secluded, hidden from the neighbours by tall brick walls and an old outhouse.

Tony dragged the corpse towards it and opened the door.

Inside were racks of tools and equipment which would make butchers and carpenters quiver with delight and serial killers shiver with anticipation.

With all the monsters he had endured, Tony had never suspected this eccentric old man might be the worst of them all.

Three chest freezers sat at the back of the outhouse.

He dragged the body across the floor, reminding himself that he would have to come back and clean up whatever remnants it spilled.

The shit he was getting in was getting deeper and deeper.

If it wasn't for Danny, he would have handed himself in.

Things would be safer that way, for sure.

He opened the first freezer, grateful it was empty and not filled with the individually wrapped body parts he'd envisaged. Lifting the corpse was a nigh on impossible task, but somehow he managed it. It fell into the freezer headfirst. He slammed the lid shut and tried not to let the tendrils of shock creep in. He couldn't stop; if he did, he would break apart.

He forced himself away from the freezers, making a mental checklist of the things he needed to do as though they were nothing more than mundane household chores.

Next job, clean us both up and get him to hospital.

FERAL

Chapter 16

Voices woke Mortimer. The familiar murmurs of Gustav and the others.

He opened his eyes and saw the portly Ukrainian hold the door open then move aside, bowing his head with almost regal fervour as a motorised wheelchair rolled into the room.

It was big, black, and armoured, a carapace for the scrawny little beetley thing inside it.

In the chair was something that should have died a long time ago, all yellow skin and poking bone, the only thing keeping it alive its orbiting mechanical organs.

Emaciated, skeletal.

Disease fused with flesh and metal.

Mortimer had never seen Sir Jonathan Butcher in the flesh, although he knew it was through sheer stubbornness and money that the old man wasn't dead.

"It's good to meet you at last, Doctor Mortimer."

A small microphone the size and shape of a bean was poised by the man's dry purple lips. Speakers within the wheeled contraption amplified his voice. Mortimer nodded, as far as the restraints would allow. "Likewise, Sir Jonathan, although I wish the circumstances had been different."

"Yes." The old man's mouth twitched. "You made a grave mistake, didn't you?"

"I think I'm more than suffering the consequences of my actions."

"Quite possibly. It's a good job my team are cleaning up your mess, although—"

"It's not my mess!" Mortimer snapped. He wasn't the one who had brought this into the country. "It had already started before me."

"Do not interrupt me again or I shall drain every drop of your blood within the hour and have you dissected into bite-sized chunks. Do you understand?"

Mortimer nodded. There was nothing he could do, nothing he could barter with.

"I'm not a stupid man, Mortimer. I foresee great things. I know how much research you did on our specimen before he escaped. I want that to continue."

Oh, wonderful, more tests, Mortimer thought.

"I want you to continue your research." Butcher must have known what the doctor was thinking as he paused to give him room to answer.

"I will," Mortimer said, unable to hide his relief. Maybe his value had been noticed after all. "But how? How?"

"We have to wait for your transformation, but we already have our eye on a pair of infected subjects."

"You mean someone from Boxford survived?"

"Yes, children. Twins. You know, an amazing man of your profession performed some fascinating studies on sets of twins, Doctor Mortimer. I've read all about them. I hope your studies will surpass his. You'll have heard of the man to whom I refer, I'm sure."

Mortimer shook his head despite a sickening inkling that the mad old man would mention the angel of death at Auschwitz.

"Doctor Josef Mengele." Butcher smiled so hard his dry lips split, blood dripping down his virtually non-existent chin. "A contact of mine once met him. Things would have been a whole lot different if he had studied lycanthropy instead of Victor Krauss, I can tell you."

This was news to Mortimer; he knew Krauss was the one responsible for the old folk turning into werewolves but didn't know the old man had studied it. He was sure Herbert hadn't mentioned that particular piece of information. He would have remembered. "How do you know Krauss studied it?"

"The younger brother stressed as much in his original police statement, but since this incident surfaced, certain doors have been opened. I know all about Victor Krauss, Doctor Mortimer, well, everything up until he vanished from Germany whilst it was under Nazi command."

"Jesus Christ," Mortimer whispered, "how long has this been out there?"

"One wouldn't like to speculate, and to do so would be fruitless. Krauss never found out and neither shall you."

"What happens now?"

One of Butcher's bodyguards swiped a hand and dabbed blood from his lips.

Mortimer was surprised when the geriatric nodded in gratitude.

"The first phase is to get you through your transformation. My connection has created a remarkable process which will help you through this stage and it is in—"

"Wait! What?" Mortimer burst out and regretted it when one of Butcher's men drew a sidearm.

Butcher's index finger, the only part he could move aside from his mouth, pushed on the wheelchair control panel, his voice booming out of the speakers. "DO NOT INTERRUPT, DOCTOR."

"I'm sorry, I'm sorry," Mortimer pleaded, unsure the man's gun could hurt him but not wanting to test it.

"It's just that you implied that your connection is already studying lycanthropy."

Butcher's grin was a dead man's rictus. "It would seem that way, wouldn't it? All shall be revealed when you're through your transformation and have proven your worth."

"But I have a right to know."

"You have a right to do as you are told," Butcher said, increasing the volume of the speakers so even the bodyguards flinched.

Mortimer lowered his eyes in defeat.

He would do as he was told.

Butcher smiled. "There's a good dog."

He was lucky they didn't want to run the same experiments he had done on Herbert.

As much as he wanted to rip Gustav apart, Mortimer was an obliging patient.

He let him take swabs, blood, whatever he needed, without one word of protest.

Physically, he felt phenomenal, as though he could smash through walls, but he wasn't stupid.

Since Butcher had hinted that his contact had already been studying lycanthropy since the end of the Second World War, he knew he couldn't risk underestimating them or their knowledge. Sure, he could turn and tear the fat Ukrainian apart, feast on his innards, and revel in the glory of bestial slaughter, but they would probably have ways of punishing him he'd never dreamed about.

There was more than enough corruption in Mortimer's mind to understand that where people with this kind of power were concerned, it was better to comply.

Comply, build up trust, and hopefully share their successes, or at least play a part in them.

Without warning, Butcher came into the room with his entourage of bodyguards, one of whom handed Gustav a USB stick.

Mortimer studied Butcher and wondered why he hadn't infected himself yet. His machines pumped him full of drugs, kept him alive. There was technology being used in Butcher's life support system that he had only heard rumours of.

Surely, having the regenerative properties of lycanthropy to hand, Butcher would have downed the first infected blood sample like a fine malt whisky. He couldn't understand it: the man could die, quite literally at any second, and yet he had the answer to that in front of him.

Butcher pressed a few buttons on his keypad, even speech seemed too much for him at the moment, and the automated voice spoke for him whilst he appeared cadaverous behind half-closed eyelids.

"Gustav will show you a simulation of how your transformation is predicted to go. You should be grateful that we have this technology to aid you."

Mortimer leant closer to Gustav's monitor, as close as the restraints would allow, and saw a naked man being led into a room.

People in hazmat suits helped him into an opaque sarcophagus and clamped thick metal restraints around his limbs, waist, and neck. The lid closed and the tomb filled with some kind of blue-coloured liquid, gradually covering the man.

The liquid covered his face and filled the tank completely.

"How does he breathe?" Mortimer asked.

Nobody said a thing as the video played out.

Numbers on the monitor showed the temperature inside the sarcophagus dropping rapidly.

The man inside started to buck and writhe beneath the restraints as he began to change shape.

The temperature was already below zero and dropping at an impossible rate.

Hypodermic needles came from the coffin sides and stabbed into the wriggling mutation.

The temperature plummeted.

Mortimer couldn't help but laugh at the ingenuity of it.

Cryogenics.

To control a wolf transformation.

He doubted the technology was advanced enough for a human to survive but might work for something that was capable of regeneration at will.

Trapping the wolf gave the host control.

Butcher's eyes came alive at his laughter and he managed two words. "You laugh?"

Mortimer held his palms up in a peaceful gesture. "Yes. But it's not what you're thinking." He pointed at the screen. "This. This is genius."

"Soon," said Butcher, with a grin.

Chapter 17

Victor slumped against the logs, the damp stench overpowering.

The scurrying of vermin deep within the wood pile was a cacophony. He could hear their pulses racing.

The intensity of his heightened senses flooded him with sight, sounds, smell and touch. Beneath his skin, legions of writhing terrors prickled up from bones that hummed with unholy fire.

A sharp pain tore apart his abdomen and the shriek which accompanied it sounded almost animal.

He tried to remember Schäfer's words of advice.

How to survive the transformation.

It was an endurance test, a battle of wills.

Images of blood, offal, and gore-coated snow flashed in front of his eyes, visions so real he thought he might reach out and bring the semi-frozen clumps of meat to his lips.

"No," Victor screamed, and tried to conjure images of Gwen on their wedding night, when they had been young and innocent.

The image came but was immediately sullied by the wolf's corruption.

Imagery, using the knowledge already inside Victor, convinced him of sins far greater than those he had committed.

The wolf's false narrative told him that he had strangled his wife; that he had taken her virginity and her last breath at the same time.

Even though it wasn't what had happened, the horror of seeing it, feeling it, *remembering* it, weakened him.

FERAL

He felt his body convulse as something lurched inside.

He clawed handfuls of the pine-needle-sprinkled soil, screamed in silent torture as his spine realigned with a series of crunches and a snap.

Fingers tearing at his clothing, he flipped onto his back and felt something pop in his chest.

Victor knew the wolf would break him, both body and mind.

Then it would win.

The pain was unbearable.

He was defenceless against its attack; the only thing he had a chance against was the mental onslaught. As impossible a task as it seemed, Victor stopped physically fighting against the change and tried to focus. His limbs crackled and broke as they elongated and reformed, ready for his new form.

Despite the considerable pain, a small part of him was still deeply fascinated by the transformation process.

He watched his legs become thick with coarse fur and hard muscle, amazed by the sheer strength in them, amazed that they were still within his control.

Maybe it was the wolf's way of trying to convince him to give in and let it take over.

Give up and all this power will be yours.

But Victor was smart, he knew he could have it both ways.

Using the last of his physical energy, he struck out at the woodpile with both of his superhuman legs, again and again and again. The logs began to tumble before the thing in him had a chance to react. Victor closed his eyes against the avalanche of timber and tried to remember his wedding night the way it actually had been.

Victor felt the beast within him rage.

His blood was liquid fire and his muscles shrieked with metamorphic exertion.

The pain of the wolf's emergence overcame the crushing weight of the tree trunks.

He heard the canine snarls coming from his throat as it realigned into something bestial. The bones in his face shattered and his jaw crunched as it thrust outwards in a ruddy explosion. Arms that were still his, but not, thickened, grew fur and claws, and raked at the logs across his waist and hips.

Internally, Victor battled with the werewolf's protests, refusing entry to the human part of his brain.

He armed himself mentally with memories of the things he loved, his barricades impenetrable.

Gwen.

Budapest.

Their wedding night.

When they first met.

Nothing could taint those memories.

He wouldn't allow it.

As the wood came crashing down, he knew how he could move from beneath but he wanted to see just how wily his wolf was on its own.

Thick black talons gouged into the bark with ease and pushed at the heavy load as it lost its temper like a toddler having a tantrum.

It was pathetic; it had no brain for strategic thinking.

It needed him more than he needed it.

He waited for its frantic thrashing to end before seizing control.

Night fell.

His new body's breathing was laborious with near-exhaustion.

The trance-like state of being a passenger in a werewolf's body was finally over.. He could picture it huddled and defeated, sulking in the corner of his psyche.

Control returned to him; this new body was now his to use.

The mental onslaught from the beast was nothing but a curious whimper now, as Victor raised his modified arms and tested their strength. "You will not be in control," he told it. "I am your master. Obey me and you will be rewarded as I see fit, or we can both die here. If I remove these logs and you dare to cheat me, I will kill us both, I know how. I know your time for control is limited and that you may use me as a vessel to run amok. But it will end, and then so will the both of us. Do as I say and you get to live, hunt, be relatively free, although attached to a leash. The modern world is not a place for monsters but I can hide us well." Victor had no idea whether the thing inside him understood anything he said, although he did feel the alien presence weaken its hold.

"Very well." He reached up as high as he could and rolled the top log from the pile, then the next and the next. It was a simple enough puzzle for a man to solve, but not for a beast.

It took a long time to clear the wood using his newfound strength, but with each piece he removed, he felt the Lycan retreat, cower, go back to wherever it would reside between transformations.

It knew its place.

With just a thought, Victor's transformation back to human began. It was even more excruciating than the reverse. His screams tore into the night as the sensations of his shattered pelvis and legs took over.

The werewolf was either powerless to thwart the pain or refused to take away the human agony. Victor thought that it might be vengeance for being made a pet. But it wasn't long before a truce was made; the Lycan's regenerative powers were offered for free. The wolf felt Victor's pain too, for as much as Victor was the wolf, the wolf was now Victor. They were one and could be divided only in death.

FERAL

Chapter 18

Doctor Charlotte Smith pushed the staffroom door open and headed straight for the drinks machine in the staffroom.

She poked the buttons without looking. She couldn't wait for her end-of-shift coffee. The bus ride home was something she dreaded, but after working twelve hours she was too tired to even think about driving. It was just after seven and she hadn't taken the twins the PPE that she'd promised. She hoped there would still be time before they dropped off to sleep.

Charlotte took her coffee and headed towards the children's ward. She was surprised to see the hospital governor at such a late hour. He walked past her escorted by four men in suits.

When he noticed her, he stopped. "Doctor Smith. May I have your files on the twins you're treating, please?"

"Yes, of course," she said, resisting the urge to ask why. She wondered who the other guys were and had a sneaking suspicion that her patients were about to be taken from her. She jogged to her nearby office to retrieve the children's files.

"Is this everything?" the governor asked, snatching the files and handing them to one of the men.

"Yeah."

"Okay. That will be all, thank you. The children are to be taken to a private clinic tonight."

Typical.

She had discovered some interesting properties in the twins' DNA and someone of a higher authority was taking the kids off her hands. "Can I say goodbye to them?"

The governor frowned; such sentiment was abnormal to him. He looked to one of the suited men, who gave a nod.

Charlotte led the five men to the children's ward, where the lights were dimmed ready for the night shift.

A nurse was busy administering the last doses of medication to those that needed it.

Visiting hours had ended half an hour before; several kids still snivelled and whined for their parents but the twins were lucky, they had each other.

Charlotte saw them lying down, ready for sleep.

Kayleigh sat up and smiled when she crept into the room. "Hello, Doctor Charlotte."

"Hey, Kayleigh," Charlotte said, sitting on her bed. "Hey, Kiran."

Kiran sat up and looked at the coffee cup in her hands. "Where are our face masks?"

"I'm sorry, I forgot all about them," she lied.

"Who are they?" Kayleigh whispered, eyeing the men in the corridor.

Charlotte smiled. "The one in the grey suit is my boss. I'm not sure who the others are."

"Why are they here?" Kiran asked.

"Well, I'm afraid they're moving you to another hospital."

Both children were horrified. Kiran eyeballed her with open-mouthed shock and Kayleigh shook her head from side to side and her little fist clutched at the blankets.

"It's okay. Everything will be fine," Charlotte said, trying to reassure them, "I've just come to say goodbye."

"Where's our mum?" Kayleigh whimpered.

"That's a good point," she muttered, and as the governor and four men entered the room, she turned to them. "Is their mother going with them on the transfer? It's protocol."

The governor stepped forward and smiled awkwardly at the kids. "I spoke to your mother this evening just after she left. She's gone home now to get some rest but she's promised she'll see you at the new hospital tomorrow."

The twins looked at each other, knowingly.

"We're not going anywhere without our mum," Kiran said stubbornly, folding his arms and staring directly at the governor with a scrutiny beyond his years.

Charlotte smiled at them, impressed, but turned her grin to one of faux sympathy toward the governor and the men.

He looked flummoxed, whereas the men remained stony-faced.

One whispered into the governor's ear and Charlotte saw the colour drain from his face.

He cleared his throat, but try as he might, he couldn't disguise his nervousness.

"How about if Doctor Charlotte were to accompany you both?"

Charlotte made to protest, shocked that he had asked without even consulting her, but she saw the twins relax and nod excitedly.

"It's okay, Doctor," one of the men said, "everything you need will be provided at the facility."

Something weird was going on, and Charlotte's hackles were more than a little raised.

No way was she going anywhere with the men unless she knew where, regardless of her feelings toward Kayleigh and Kiran.

Charlotte stared at the governor in disbelief. "You can't just expect me to drop ev—"

"Look," he squirmed, a nervous grin touching his lips, "if you aren't capable of going at such a short notice I fully understand. Maybe I can find an older, more experienced—"

"No, I'll go. I'll go," she said, deliberately cutting through his words as he had hers. "But this just doesn't feel right."

His laugh was patronising. "This isn't a top-secret government conspiracy, Charlotte. You've been watching too many episodes of the X-Files. All this is is the Private Medical Health Sector offering to help out with something that's been flagged up as unique."

"You mean so they can benefit from it?"

The governor sighed. "So we can all benefit from it. But mostly so things get done quicker."

Charlotte eyed the four men standing sentry outside the room. Nurses rushed in and out getting everything ready for the twins to be transferred. Despite how she felt about all this, she could only think about Kiran and Kayleigh's little faces and their fear of being shipped off without their mother.

One of the four men made eye contact with the governor and nodded.

The governor turned and offered the same false smile. "Time to go, Charlotte."

Chapter 19

Boxford was alive with news vans and emergency vehicles commingling with the heavy police presence which had taken over the park.

Juliet's bus pulled past the Victorian garden, police cordons at every entrance. The clean-up after the events which had put Boxford on the map would take ages. She expected a phone call at any second to tell her they had found her father's remains.

The bus pulled into the station. She shuffled down the aisle ready to venture out into the night. A few copies of the local free newspaper littered the floor and the seats.

The headline made her stop.

MASS FUNERAL PYRE IN PARK.

"Oh, Jesus."

"You alright, love?" said a man behind her.

She didn't reply other than to point a shaking finger at the newspaper headline.

"Terrible, ain't it?" he said, squeezing past her. "Bloody gangs. Ain't safe to go outside nowadays."

"They are saying it was gangs?"

"Yeah. Bloody lunatics running amok in costumes. Some kind of turf war, they reckon, with a group from Sudbury."

It made more sense than werewolves, although it didn't explain her father's involvement, and it certainly didn't explain what was happening with the twins.

The Green Man estate was deserted, a rare sight at any time of the day, no matter how cold the weather.

There was police tape everywhere and now one of the ground floor flats was boarded up.

Juliet pressed her key fob to the lock and went into the building.

"Hold up, love," a woman called, trotting up the access ramp.

Juliet turned and held the door for the young blonde, who was carrying a fast-food courier's bag.

The sudden smell of hot food made Juliet nauseated.

She let the courier go ahead and watched her vanish into the foyer.

When she got to the nearest lift, she saw it had already begun its slow climb. "It's okay, I'll get the other one." Juliet rolled her eyes and followed the foyer around toward the farthest lift.

The safety lights had been vandalised yet again and the small hall was only lit by the green of the fire exit sign.

She entered the darkened foyer between the lifts and got another whiff of the greasy takeaway food, something garlicky. Then an arm slipped around her chest and something cold pressed against her throat.

*

Charlotte followed the governor through the hospital.

Two of the suited men pushed the twins in wheelchairs.

Everyone seemed in a rush.

None of it felt right, even less so when she mentioned phoning the twins' mother to let her know about the transfer and her suggestion was immediately dismissed.

"Let it wait until the morning," the governor said as they neared the car park.

They left the hospital and the group of men headed to a black van with darkened windows.

"Who the hell are you guys?" Charlotte asked one of the men, who shrugged and smiled. They opened the rear of the van and someone pressed a few buttons on a small remote. A platform unfolded itself from out of nowhere and lowered towards the ground.

"Cool," Kiran said as one of the men pushed his chair onto the lift.

Charlotte took the opportunity to take her phone out to ring Juliet.

"There are no phone calls to be made in the vehicle. All mobile devices must be switched off."

She looked at the man incredulously.

"Jesus, really? What next, are you going to drug me so I don't see the location of your top-secret hideout?"

The man gave a wry smile and slid a hand inside his jacket. "Yes."

Charlotte sprang back.

He pulled his empty hand back out and waggled his fingers at her. "Relax, doctor. There's nothing to worry about. We just have some special monitoring equipment on board."

Charlotte choked on laughter. "You absolute cretin. I honestly believed you for a second."

"Try not to worry, Doctor." He smiled, his teeth as immaculate as the rest of him. "If you need to make a phone call, please do it now; but be quick, as we have a tight schedule and a good two hours' drive."

Charlotte gave him a thumbs-up and laughed as Kayleigh started rising on the van lift. "You pair are getting the royalty treatment, aren't you?"

She heard Kiran ask one of the men if they could stop by a drive-thru McDonald's on the way to wherever it was they were going.

She pointed to her phone. "Just going to let your mum know you're on the way."

Charlotte tapped buttons and waited for the call to connect. It rang twice before she heard Juliet scream, "Help me, someone's attacking me!"

Chapter 20

Bartholomew couldn't remember anything about going to the hospital other than a corridor full of abstract art and rushing people, but he was there alright. Except he wasn't alright.

There was a dark shadow over the vision in his right eye.

Before the hospital, he'd still had vision in it, although no control over its slackened mechanics.

Tony had taken too long to tidy things up before getting him to the hospital.

There was no room for fear or anger.

Bartholomew accepted the cards fate had dealt him and tried to figure out just how severe the situation was.

He was on a ward with men in different stages of decrepitude.

There was no sign of anyone in a uniform that didn't belong in a hospital, which hopefully meant his little assistant hadn't dobbed him in.

He didn't think the brothers would make another run for it; Tony had made it obvious they had nowhere to go.

They were now at one another's mercy.

Bartholomew saw the remote to summon the nurses and pressed the button in order to find out how bad things really were.

*

The silence and inactivity did his head in.
Not having a window did his head in.
Everything did his head in.

He couldn't survive this way, neither of them could. It was worse than being in prison.

Some of Danny's older acquaintances he knew through the GMC claimed being in the nick wasn't bad if you kept yourself to yourself and could hold your own in a scuffle.

With Tony having gone to help his friend, Danny was alone with his thoughts and they were taking him down dark avenues. The urge to hand himself in was getting stronger. He got as far as trying the back door but Tony had locked him in. He had been gone for hours and Danny was worried that something must have happened.

What if he had been seen and recognised, despite his change of appearance?

Would he tell the cops where they were hiding, or would he cover?

What if something worse had happened?

What if he'd been hurt resisting arrest?

Danny went through the provisions Tony's mate had brought them, calculating how many days the food on the coffee table would last him.

About four days, tops.

Danny picked the diary up and leafed through the pages, wondering why his mate had included it in the first place.

Something grabbed his attention.

Little circles in the corners of intermittent pages showed the cycle of the moon.

Was this the reason for the diary?

Had Tony asked for it?

He flicked through the pages to find out when the next full moon was due and noticed a spidery scrawl filling up some of the dates. Nothing deep and meaningful, just names, times, appointments, by the look of things.

When he saw his brother's name on the following day's entry alongside a man's, it temporarily distracted him from what he was searching for.

A sinking feeling told Danny that what his brother was into was a lot worse than he had suspected.

Checking the bedrooms of the house and finding a bedside cabinet full of condoms and sex toys confirmed it.

This was a fucking knocking shop.

His brother was working in a brothel.

Danny burst back into the living room and booted the coffee table.

He picked the diary up and began to tear pages out, only pausing when he saw his own name jotted down beside the name Bartholomew and a tiny full moon symbol.

*

Tony went over the hallway and bathroom again and scrubbed at the deep-pile carpet. After repeatedly going at the bloodstains the water from the sponge finally came away clean.

There was nothing else he could do.

He took the cheap phone he had been given and dialled the emergency services, making sure to withhold the number.

"There's a man, he's had a stroke," he said before telling them the address, and hid down the side of the boarded-up house opposite Tepes' property.

He took the ring of Tepes' keys from his pocket and let himself in through the back. The man's house had been his parents'; the garden looked like an old builder's yard, with small archaic, red-bricked buildings in various states of dilapidation.

Along the wall hung black-and-white photographs of Tepes as a child: there was no mistaking his dark features, posing beside a builder's truck that bore a merchant's name Tony didn't recognise.

A tall, muscular man with a moustache and fierce countenance stood with his arm around him, hand gripping his shoulder as though he was holding him in place.

Other photos showed various landscapes, perhaps taken on holiday, snapshots of an older Tepes with a woman Tony presumed was his mother. In these photos, it was Tepes holding *her* in place.

At the top of the stairs hung a large colour portrait, which appeared to have been professionally done, depicting Tepes in a dark suit, his hair slicked back into a ponytail, staring intently into the camera with the merest hint of a smile. In one hand, he held a glass of red wine aloft.

Tony hated himself for noticing just how attractive the man was.

He was a manipulating monster, never to be underestimated.

Just minutes before, after he had cleaned for the second time, his newly acquired phone rang.

With extreme reluctance, he answered.

"Hi, my name's Steve, I'm a nurse at Sudbury General, am I speaking to Daniel Oram?"

"No, I think you've got the wrong number…"

"Your uncle isn't Bartholomew Tepes?"

"Shit, sorry, ummm yeah, it is. Err, sorry, I'm not very good on the phone, I have…"

"It's all good," the nurse said, "your uncle warned me of your social anxiety."

He went on to explain what had happened, in which Tony did a decent job of faking sincerity and shock, and requested he bring to the hospital a list of things which he would find in a bag upstairs, like an expectant mother's hospital kit.

Tony couldn't argue.

Whatever state Tepes was in, he was capable of communication, capable of being his usual devious self. He had Tony and Danny firmly by the balls.

Tony found a large leather holdall in a cupboard at the top of the stairs, exactly where the nurse had said it would be, next to Tepes' bedroom.

A vast king-size bed draped in black and red sheets dominated the room, unmade.

Everything else was black.

The bag was filled with several days' worth of clothing, like it was packed ready to grab and run.

In a bedside cabinet, he found a toiletry bag and went to find the bathroom.

Two of the doors he tried were locked and he left them that way.

Behind the third door was the bathroom. He studied his reflection in the medicine cabinet before rifling through it for things Tepes might need.

He hated the dull brown hair dye he'd used, and the crooked haircut he'd done himself made him look like a degenerate.

He wondered if he would ever get to be himself again.

He threw the toiletries onto the mattress and swore as a packet of razor blades dropped to the carpet. He knelt down to retrieve them and stopped when he saw three metal briefcases under the bed.

"Oh, shit." He recoiled as though they were suspect bombs.

His instinct told him to leave them well alone, that someone as crooked as Tepes would not be keeping anything legal in such containers, but he was pulling them out from the dark confines before he even knew what he was doing.

Further surprises came when he saw that the cases weren't combination-locked.

He searched through Tepes' keys until he found three little ones that looked as though they might fit.

"Please don't be drugs," Tony whispered and slid one of the keys in. A tiny red LED flickered on and off as the mechanism clicked, and his blood ran cold, thinking he had activated some hi-tech booby trap.

Holding his breath, as though it could save him from potential explosion, he lifted the lid.

The case was full of neatly stacked twenty-pound notes.

No wires, no poisonous gases.

His heart leapt into his throat.

The second case was crammed with identity cards, student passes, driving licences, bank cards.

Almost all of them bore photographs of young men.

Tony wondered if the one he had loaded into the freezer was the last in a long line, or whether this wasn't the serial killer's trophy stash it seemed to be.

He closed the case and opened the third.

More money, in numerous currencies, a sandwich bag full of little hexagonal green pills and a handgun — with ammunition.

Tony closed the cases and sat against the bed, every fibre of his being screaming at him to take the money and run.

A small part even considered doing it without Danny, who, in a matter of days, would turn into a monster and potentially start all this shit off again, all because he hadn't had the nerve to kill him when he'd had the chance.

Tony thought about the gun in the case, it would probably be useless against his brother now.

But what if Danny could learn to control it, or be forced to control it?

He thought of the cellar in Tepes' brothel.

Billy wasn't due back from Thailand for another fortnight.

Billy ran his tricks from the basement.

Tony had only been down there the once, it was for high-paying customers who were into specialist, very specific stuff.

Billy was the resident dominatrix there, and he was a fucking bitch. He had gathered illegal tools and toys from his annual sabbaticals, no doubt funded by Tepes.

Tony knew there was enough equipment down there to restrain his brother but he didn't know if it would be strong enough to hold the monster he would become.

But if it did, and if he had the money ready, and Tepes remained incapacitated in hospital, they would be able to get a month's head start before it happened again.

They could get anywhere in a month.

They had to do it.

It was their only chance at even trying to start a new life somewhere else. All they had to do was ride out Danny's first transformation.

Part 2

FERAL

Chapter 21
1945

Days, maybe weeks, who knew? Time seemed to be distorted amidst Victor's agonising delirium.

He felt hunger pangs grow from subtle aches to stomach-tearing wrenches as he was rebuilt anew, piece-by-piece.

Sustenance came eventually.

After wetting his lips on melting snow whilst waiting for his body to repair itself, his immobility attracted inquisitive —but unfortunate— woodland creatures.

Slowly, he was able to move, the pain lessening day by day.

Victor knew he was almost healed.

When he finally resurfaced, the snow had gone, melted from the valley, where he had lain for what felt like months, a hibernating bear. His clothes were ragged and he was black with filth. Around him lay the pelts and skins of rabbits, squirrels, and other small rodents. Some he had caught using the wolf's unnatural speed as they came to inspect what looked —and probably smelled—like a dead body.

Now he was a man reborn.

He felt younger than he had in decades, his senses were heightened, and there was a new level of consciousness. A desire to rid himself of the rotten rags and bask in the winter sun, plant his feet in cold soil and absorb the nutrients as if he were a tree.

He hoped that wherever Gwen was, she felt as glorious as he did.

Visions of what he had done to the Schäfer children still haunted him.

The memory of his betrayal and the subsequent guilt would never, ever leave him.

If only there had been another way.

The Schäfers weren't mankillers other than for their own survival. They were never maneaters. They knew the importance of never letting their wolves consume the flesh of man.

Victor found it hard to believe such a thing as lycanthropy had managed to die down to just one family of four, though.

There must be others out there living similar lives of seclusion.

It was that line of thinking which had helped him decide to steal their gift and get away from Germany.

The tang of blood brought him from his reverie. He allowed his wolf to follow the scent through several miles of pines until the trees thinned out and he came to a field.

On the grass lay dozens of sheep, their thick winter fleeces dark crimson where something had gone at them.

A farmer and a farm-hand worked beside a tractor, dragging the corpses towards a trailer.

Victor crouched to inspect the closest body. The lifeless animal's throat had been shredded to the point of near decapitation. One next to it was a hollowed-out mess.

Angry voices barked across the field in German.

A shotgun was pointed in his direction.

Victor raised his hands and slowly stood; this seemed to alarm the two men even more.

Then he remembered his appearance.

Dishevelled, filthy, ragged clothing, dried animal blood.

"Lycan!" the farmer cried and blasted his gun.

Victor fell to the ground, even though the shot had missed, but the men were racing across the field.

He scrambled back up and ran into the confines of the pine forest.

FERAL

Chapter 22

Sensation.

Bartholomew thanked whichever demon watched over him for the return of feelings in his left arm and the vision in his left eye.

Before, a doctor had waffled techno-babble about the latest in medical procedures for stroke victims, and he had simply slurred, 'Do it.' His queer little Renfield had showed up just before the end of visiting hours with everything on his list. *Bless his heart.*

Like a frightened rabbit, Tony had crept into the hospital with his newly dyed hair and several days' worth of facial stubble. In comparison with how well-groomed the lad had been before, it was a subtle but effective disguise.

Neither of them said a lot.

It was a simple transaction: Tony brought Bartholomew's essentials, stayed for five minutes for the sake of appearances, then left.

However, before he departed, Bartholomew made certain the boy had connected his phone to the charger. Communication would be easier that way for now. Although barely a word was offered between the two when Tony left the hospital, Bartholomew sent him a message telling him not to think about going anywhere or to even consider slacking on his duties at the whorehouse.

He was still in charge.

After initially ignoring the number of trivial alerts and notifications one normally gets after having their phone off for several hours, the boredom of lying in a room of geriatrics got the better of him.

He spotted the keyhole-shaped alert immediately and felt his pulse speed up.

The fucking prying little shit.

He cursed himself for not getting cases with combination locks, he'd thought he was going one better by getting locks that could be tracked by GPS, which would alert his mobile phone if they were tampered with.

Bartholomew thought about what was in those two cases and tried to predict how the boys would react.

He was almost certain that the persona he had presented to the older Scarborough brother instilled a healthy dose of fear, but whether it was enough to stop him from double-crossing him to save his younger brother was another thing.

If he told Tony he knew his cases had been opened, then the brothers might bolt and take everything, but they could be doing that anyway.

Bartholomew cursed his bad luck.

He needed to get out of the hospital but didn't have the first idea how.

Weighing up the pros and cons of telling Tony about the cases exhausted him so he sent one more warning message and let fate decide.

Bartholomew placed his phone on the bed beside him and thought about blood.

He closed his eyes and envisaged the vein bulging out from the top of Tony's shirt collar.

*

Don't worry about me, I'm in the best place, as they say. Ha, ha. Oh, and by the way, I have several people watching the house, keeping an eye on you pair, just to make sure you're all safe and secure.

Tony thrust the mobile phone back into his pocket and hurried back to his brother.

*

Danny dropped the diary but the little black circle remained in his head.

That was how much time he had left until he turned into one of those things.

He needed to go whilst Tony was out.

Run off on his own.

At least he wouldn't kill his own fucking brother that way.

He could feel it inside him.

His own body was becoming stronger by the day and it scared the hell out of him.

Tony's hair in the bathroom bin showed him just a fraction of what his brother had sacrificed for his protection.

Danny picked up a pair of nail scissors from the sink and tested their points. A cold detachment came over him as his reflection seemed to take over. It nodded to him and he began to remove his clothes, mirroring his reflection's movements rather than the other way around.

Once naked, he got in the bath and sat down.

There would be less mess that way.

Without even pausing to consider what he was about to do, Danny pushed the scissor blades into the prominent veins on his left forearm and dragged them towards his wrist.

*

Even after all the blood he had mopped up at Tepes' place, even after all the death and destruction he had already witnessed, Tony still threw up when he entered the bathroom and saw the arterial sprays decorating the tiled walls.

Danny lay naked in the bathtub.

The water was red. So, so red.

Two deep, jagged gouges spread apart the flesh on both of his forearms. A broken pair of bloodied scissors lay on the saturated bathmat.

"They heal as fast as I make them," Danny managed to choke out, before slamming his head against the shattered tiles behind him.

Tony grabbed a towel from the rack and went to his brother's aid. Danny was right: the cuts were healing right before his eyes. The bleeding slowed to a trickle and the open flesh slowly knitted back together.

Neither of them spoke, words wouldn't come. For the first time in their lives, all their defences were down. They embraced and gave into the tears and the utter hopelessness of their situation.

Chapter 23

Everyone, it seemed, had a fitness tracker; people were obsessed with measuring and recording everything.

When her eldest, Jeanelle, bought her one for her birthday and linked it to her mobile and headphones, Juliet had thought it was ridiculous.

Modern technology made people lazy.

However, the convenience of hands-free phone calls was something she soon found herself getting on board with.

That she could answer her phone without removing it from her bag or pocket with just a press of the wrist device was a godsend.

Her attacker didn't know she had answered a call, had just thought she was calling for help from anyone who was listening.

Juliet drove her elbow back, felt it connect with something soft, and heard what she supposed was a knife clatter to the floor.

She ran towards the lit area by the lift, screaming like a banshee.

Whoever had called her had said her name; she recognised the voice: Kiran and Kayleigh's doctor.

Her immediate thoughts were that something had happened to her babies. *They don't call at this time of night for nothing.* Panic threatened to overwhelm her.

She hammered against the doors opposite the lift despite knowing that most of the ground floor flats had been empty for some time.

The courier bolted around the corner and swung a fist at her jaw.

FERAL

Juliet's head snapped sideways, her head connected with the lift doors, and she fell to the ground.

*

"Hello, hello?" Charlotte yelled into the phone.

There was the sound of a brief struggle before a loud metallic clang cut the call off.

"Is everything okay?" asked the man who was closing the back of the van.

Charlotte dragged him away out of the twins' earshot.

"I just rang their mum, she said she was being attacked."

Surprise covered his face for a few seconds before he regained composure. "Get in the van and we'll get someone there as soon as possible. Give me your phone."

Charlotte handed over the phone without hesitation and got in the back with Kiran and Kayleigh.

The man beckoned to the driver as the other two piled in with Charlotte and the kids.

They exchanged words, and the driver pulled out a phone, making a quick call whilst reading information from Charlotte 's.

"What is happening?" she asked.

The driver turned and smiled. "I've sent someone to help immediately, don't worry. Everything will be taken care of."

"But how?"

"We have more reliable connections than the police, Doctor." His eyes lit up on sight of the twins. "Someone will be able to get to the bottom of this within a few minutes." He started the van and pulled away from the hospital.

"Can I have my phone back?"

"Of course," the driver said, although he made no attempt to offer her the device. "But, as I said, no phones are allowed in the vehicle."

"So, how are you going to hear from your connections?"

"What's going on, Doctor Charlotte?" Kayleigh said suspiciously.

Charlotte forced a smile.

"Doctor Charlotte," the driver piped up, "was just worried the ice cream machine in McDonald's might be broken. I told her I'd get someone to phone ahead and check."

*

Juliet was on the floor. In front of her, the lift doors opened and she felt herself being dragged inside.

A smash.

Fragments of glass rained down on her head and shoulders.

The CCTV camera.

Her head swam with the impact of striking the metal door.

The courier jabbed a finger at the top button in the lift. She rolled Juliet onto her back and straddled her chest.

Juliet tried to wriggle free but her arms were pinned to her sides by the woman's strong thighs. "Please," she begged.

The woman placed a hand on her chest and brought the knife towards her once more.

"I have children."

"This is nothing personal," the courier said, and pushed the blade against Juliet's neck.

She squirmed beneath the knife but there was nowhere to go.

She whimpered and waited to die.

The lift doors opened and a shocked man's voice shouted, "What the bloody hell?" and from the landing, a walking stick was thrust into the courier's chest.

Juliet scooted back, out of the lift.

Before the woman had a chance to right herself, Juliet threw the first punch she had ever thrown in her life — and it was a good one.

The woman slammed into the rear wall of the lift and slid toward the floor just as the doors began to close and the car continued its upward journey.

Juliet turned to her saviour, a middle-aged man in a hi-vis jacket. A mess of grey hair burst out at random angles from beneath a flat cap.

She instantly recognised him, a resident loner on the estate who had been there as long as she had, if not longer. The local kids called him *Pete the Paedo* purely because he was weird-looking, reclusive, and dressed in what her dad presumed were his dead father's clothes. Juliet didn't care. She flung her arms around him and watched as the lift ascended.

Chapter 24
1945

Victor was able to heighten his sense of hearing by concentrating hard. Thinking about nothing else, he closed his eyes.

The farmer and farmhand were tracking him through the pines, their footfalls as loud as thunder. He could smell them, hear their hearts crashing.

He sped up, fully utilising the new energies he had acquired, courtesy of the beast inside him.

He had no desire to hunt these men; they had already suffered enough with the loss of their flock.

Victor knew he was somewhere east of Offenburg and thought if Gwen was alive it was likely she would be headed somewhere populated.

"Okay, let's see what you're capable of."

Victor focused on his hands, urging them to change.

Nothing happened to begin with.

He held them out, staring at their filthy backs, then a spark of intense, cold pain shot through the centre of each palm and spidered outwards along his fingers and thumbs and deep into his wrists and forearms.

The fine bones crackled like twigs on a fire and the skin darkened as it stretched and rippled. His fingernails split, his fingers elongated, and dark black claws burst through the disturbed cuticles.

The pain was agonising but mesmerising.

The scientist in him studied the change with fascination. It was like he was wearing the gloves of a monster. They no doubt looked ridiculous on such a shrivelled up old man.

The low voices of the two men were getting closer.

Victor moved toward the nearest tree. All the ones in this part of the forest were colossal things, rising up forty, fifty feet. His claws sunk into the bark with ease. It was the first time he had climbed a tree since he was a child, and even then, it had never been so easy. He pulled himself up the trunk, his modified hands wet with sap and drying blood, and thrust himself deep into the dark confines of the branches, hugging the trunk like a lover.

The two men passed by without noticing him, looking down for his trail.

The farmer pointed to something farther down the path into the forest.

Victor's heart stopped: he saw something move.

What had he missed?

The farmer knelt to examine a heap of disturbed foliage.

Something had passed through this way just before them.

Victor tried to look through the close-knit trees. A fleeting glimpse, something far away, moving, gone as quickly as it had appeared.

The sheep, some of the blood had been wet. Even though he guessed Gwen might have gone this way, he didn't think it would have been so recent.

"Oh God," Victor whispered, "Gwen."

He began to crawl back down the tree as quietly as he could.

As Victor climbed down, he managed to get a better look at the person ahead of the farmer and his helper.

An emaciated, blood-covered woman.

Gwen.

There was no time for stealthy manoeuvre; Victor flung himself from the tree, amazed by the power he held.

He collided with another tree, used one of his adapted hands to dig into the trunk, and pivoted himself in the direction of the two men.

The farmer raised his gun.

Victor fell behind him, raking his claws down the farmer's back as he landed.

The farmer collapsed and the shot fired up into the treetops.

The farmhand spun around to confront him.

"I'm sorry," Victor managed before driving a fist into the young man's face. He meant to knock him unconscious, but the sound his neck made when his head snapped back told him he'd done much more.

The farmer crawled across the forest floor, grabbed his gun, and rolled over onto his shredded back.

Victor grabbed the gun barrel as the farmer pulled the trigger, and felt his stomach explode.

He flew back against a tree and felt the beast inside him surfacing, begging to take over.

He let it.

As he shrieked with the pain of the gutshot, his cranium split and his jaw shattered.

His mouth was filled with gritty slush as human teeth made way for canine.

On the ground, the farmer fought against his own agonies and attempted to reload his shotgun. Victor, still in control of his rapidly changing body, fell on the farmer and buried his newly-formed wolf snout in his hot guts. He tore through the layers of clothing. The farmer's sweat saturated everything, then he was through the skin and into the glorious wet offal.

The farmer's screams, the beating of his fists, both were swamped by the taste and texture of the feeding. It absorbed almost every ounce of him, was powerful enough to take full control if he were to let it, which he would have done if the figure they were pursuing hadn't chosen that moment to poke her head out from behind a tree.

Chapter 25

The hours after Danny's perpetual suicide attempts passed by in a blur of cold, grey desperation. Tony came clean about what the house was used for, what *he* was used for, and how Tepes had lured him into his slimy network.

"But there's a way out," he added hastily, before their mood could sink to even lower depths.

"How?" Danny asked, studying his healed arms.

Tony told him about Tepes' stash: the money, the drugs, the gun, and the trophy case of likely victims.

"He'll come after us. He'll kill us."

"Yeah. But we'll be long gone by the time he gets better," Tony said. "*If* he gets better."

Danny blazed with something other than dread, a fire behind his eyes. "What if we took his stuff and then grassed him up whilst he's still in hospital?"

Tony was amazed by his brother's ingenuity.

Danny pulled a sheet of crumpled paper from his pocket. "Full moon is tomorrow night."

"Have you been in the basement yet?"

"No, why?"

"It's a bondage dungeon."

Danny leapt up from his seat. "You aren't locking me in there!"

"There's enough equipment down there to hopefully keep you restrained. It's not as if I'm going to leave you gagged and bound with a massive buttplug stuck up your arse."

"You can fuck right off with that shit."

"It might give you something else to focus on aside from turning into a werewolf."

Danny sniggered. "You're a twat, do you know that?"

Tony nodded.

"What if the restraints don't work?"

"I don't know," Tony said, "I was thinking maybe I could see if there was something in Tepes' stuff that would knock you out, not physically, like with a baseball bat, but medically."

"So, basically tie me up and get me off my fucking tits?"

Tony snorted. "Doesn't sound like a bad night."

"Dude, I'm your brother." Danny grimaced but at least the sick humour was lightening the mood. "What if all that fails?"

"Then I guess it'll have to be the buttplug." Tony reached out and took Danny's hands. "Look, we're in this together, Dan. I'm not going to bail out on you."

Danny flopped back onto the sofa and let the paper slip from his fingers. It landed face down, revealing on the back a name in Tepes' scrawl. Danny read it. "Who's Cyril?"

Cyril counted the notes the ATM spat at him and stuffed them into his pocket. A small mustard Nissan hatchback sat idling on the road.

He got in the driver's side, no small feat for someone six-and-a-half feet tall. When seated, his beige chinos rode halfway up his shins, uncovering argyle socks and brown loafers. He rolled his bulbous blue eyes towards the mirrors and stretched an arm across his chest to grab the seat belt.

He switched the ignition on; The Bee Gees continued to sing one of their classics.

Two teenagers smirked at him as they passed by, either at him or his choice in music; probably both.

He caught his sneering reflection in the rear-view mirror; his teeth were too tiny and grey.

He wiped a shaking hand over his sweaty head and pulled away from the pavement.

Cyril hated mirrors, loathed his reflection; despised the body he was in. He considered himself out of proportion, deformed.

He did have a ridiculously small head for someone so bloody big, limbs that went on forever, and the older he got, the more ghoulish he thought he looked.

An alien-human hybrid. A pale-skinned, clammy, walking cadaver with a hairless dome for a head.

All his life he had taken up so much physical space but hardly anyone really *saw* him or knew him.

Sweat soaked the armpits of his shirt.

Rather than unfasten the buttons, which he always kept fastened right to the top, he unwound the window. "Hope you like The Bee Gees," he sniggered in his nowhere accent.

Despite moving around quite a lot as a kid, he had never picked up any regional lilts.

He'd never had friends then, not only because his parents moved around so much, but also because he was strange.

When his father killed himself, he just gave up trying when it came to other people.

The traffic lights changed to red and he slowed the car to a stop. The two lads who had laughed at him were coming up level with the car. He saw them nudge each other and laugh again.

They looked like students; there were always a lot of them around at this time of day.

They had matching face fuzz to make themselves look older. One of them held the straps of his backpack and started strutting along the path like John Travolta in Stayin' Alive. Cyril liked the way his hoody strained across his chest, and his slightly effeminate jawline.

He imagined wrapping his hand around that neck and felt himself grow hard.

The boys walked by the car, and the dancer made a finger-gun at him and winked.

For a second, Cyril allowed himself to be fooled into thinking this was a sign of genuine approval, but then both boys burst into laughter and walked into a shop on the corner. Cyril hated himself even more in that moment, that one single moment in which he entertained the idea they might have thought him cool, or *sick*, or whatever it was the kids called it nowadays.

"Fuck you," he yelled into the rear-view mirror, as the drivers behind beeped their horns at the green light.

He switched off the music and sped away, muttering obscenities and wallowing in self-hatred.

Cyril parked his glob of pus outside Bartholomew's house.

He never drove to any of the brothels, or *workhouses*, as Bartholomew referred to them.

He couldn't wait to see Tony; he was amazed it had been only a month since his last visit.

He wanted to do everything with him this time, spend the night.

Last time, he'd only been able to afford Tony to take him in his mouth.

It wasn't enough.
He needed to be with him.
Entirely.
To be naked.

To hold and be held by him, for as long as his money could enable.

It had been a long time since he had been this obsessed with anyone.

He knew his feelings weren't reciprocated, but Tony was very good at making him believe they were. And at least he could get the things he wanted without resorting to the measures he had used in the past.

He would kill himself before he went back to prison.

The time he had done in the eighties for selling child pornography — not the worst of his crimes but the worst he was caught for — had nearly killed him.

People, both inside and outside of jail, did not tolerate people like him.

If they ever found out about Samuel and the others, he would be put away forever.

Samuel Ellington had been his first infatuation.

A tall, handsome lad with a mess of Robert Plant curls the colour of fire. The dead spit of Rory Gallagher.

Everyone had long hair then; even Cyril, before premature balding made that look ridiculous.

He had driven a bright-red Vauxhall Firenza back then; all the kids loved it, thought he was cool. It was the only time in his adult life that he had ever been popular.

They liked him because he was older, played all the latest music, and could get his hands on pretty much anything their little hearts desired.

All Samuel wanted was booze and fags, the usual stuff.

Everything was fine until Cyril got him alone in his car and grabbed his thigh.

Cyril insisted he was joking, managed to keep the kid quiet for weeks with free stuff, but he just got greedier and greedier, and Cyril became more and more frustrated.

Samuel's life came to an end in a layby near Bluebell Woods in the back of the Firenza.

Bluebell Woods was vast, and as a nature reserve, left pretty much alone aside from the odd official path here and there.

Over the decades, Cyril planted at least three of his infatuations deep beneath the pretty blue flowers.

Quite often, late at night, he would drive through the woods and imagine his boys running through the trees, happy now they were free from life's traumas, but he would never revisit their actual graves.

It was a long time since that special kind of urge had presented itself; he thought, maybe stupidly, that he had grown out of it.

Oh, rape and serial-killing? Grown out of it, mate. Was a passing fad, you know how it is.

But something about Tony had awakened a part he thought was extinct.

He had unleashed almost every one of his urges upon the boy but there were some things people wouldn't let you do, even for money. However, since hearing about Tony and his younger brother's fugitive status, the older, more primal compulsion had resurfaced.

*

Bartholomew placed his phone back on the bed.

"Thank God for Cyril." He chose to say the words aloud to test his speech.

Thank God for Cyril.

He had known Cyril for several years; he couldn't remember how many, exactly, but it was long before he started renting out boys.

Bartholomew supposed that if you were to look at things from an outsider's point of view, Cyril might be said to be a friend, or the closest someone like him would ever get to having a friend.

Worried that the stroke had damaged his memory, he forced himself to recall how they first met. It took a while but the answer eventually came when he saw one of the other patients pick up a magazine.

At Felixstowe market, Cyril had sold illegal pornography which he had purchased from the continent.

Despite being a grimy sleazeball of a man, Bartholomew saw him as a valuable connection and as they got to know one another, he showed a loyalty like no other.

Cyril was the true Renfield to his Dracula.

It was Cyril who acquired anything he didn't want to sully himself with. It was also Cyril who saw to the surveillance of the workhouses.

When he wasn't a patron of them.

Cyril liked them young.

Bartholomew knew what he was when he met him, knew from the things he saw him sell, but there wasn't any way he would have underage boys in his workhouses.

He didn't care about paedophilia—with his track record in serial murder it would be a tad hypocritical to have that limitation—it was just too risky to have in his business.

FERAL

If Cyril got caught doing anything like he had in the nineties, he would never see the light of day again.

All of Bartholomew's recruits worked of their own free will, and Cyril was a regular.

When Bartholomew told him Tony and his younger brother were secretly holed up there full time, he brimmed with excitement.

Tony was Cyril's latest infatuation.

He would want to do everything with the lad, and often paid extortionate amounts to spend the night with him.

When Bartholomew found out his stash had been tampered with, his first port of call had been Cyril.

The man seemed genuinely worried about his health, his concern quite touching, but he soon seized the opportunity for self-gain when Bartholomew asked him to keep an eye on the house.

Cyril wanted dibs on Tony's brother, despite being told Danny didn't work there.

Bartholomew didn't care, so he agreed.

There was no way the brothers would be leaving that place alive after all this.

Maybe, if he was strong enough, both he and Cyril could have some bloody good fun.

Chapter 26

"Are you going to be alright?" Peter asked, avoiding eye contact and beginning to fidget with the zip of his jacket. It was obvious to Juliet that the man had few skills in social interaction.

"No." There wasn't anything else she could say; someone was trying to kill her. "I need to phone the police."

Peter nodded and remained stock-still. He seemed to mull over the situation for a few more painstakingly slow seconds. "Do you want to phone from inside my flat?"

"Yes, please." Juliet nodded eagerly; the lift had reached the top floor and was now starting to come back down. "We'd better hurry."

Peter hooked his walking stick over his forearm and turned towards a blue door. "It's a mess. I don't usuall—"

"It's fine," Juliet insisted, and followed him into an L-shaped hallway. The smell of cat piss invaded her nostrils and the place felt as cold as hell. Peter switched on the light and closed the door. He continued to stand like a nervous schoolboy.

"Aren't you going to lock it?" Juliet asked, as patiently as she could manage.

"Oh, yeah," Peter said, half-dazed, and fumbled with his keys.

Juliet's phone started ringing before she could dial out, showing an unknown number. She hung up and heard Peter's front door burst open.

"Hey," he shouted, obscured by the turn in the wall, "you can't just come in he—oh."

FERAL

The way he said '*Oh*' made her hesitate.

She looked down the hallway in time to see one of his hands slap on the wall as he staggered around the corner with a knife handle sticking out of his chest, the courier right behind him.

"No," Juliet cried, as the woman pushed Peter aside and came toward her.

She turned and ran into the first room she came to. All the flats in the tower blocks were set out the same as hers, so finding the light switch in the dark room was easy.

The only downside was that Peter's place was the opposite way around. If it was her flat, this would be the kitchen instead of the lounge, where she was more likely to find something to defend herself with.

She ran to the farthest corner of the room and automatically tried the door to the balcony, even though she would be just as trapped out there.

The door was locked.

The courier stood in the doorway to the room, panting.

She had the knife again, it was slick with Peter's blood. She looked exhausted.

"Why are you doing this?" Juliet said, moving behind an old armchair, anything to buy her some time.

The woman crossed the room slowly.

There was nowhere left to run.

Peter's living room was decked out with outdated furniture: a threadbare suite, and an old sideboard covered with porcelain figurines.

Juliet picked one up at random: it felt heavy, a little boy and girl kissing.

She hurled it at the woman, who stepped aside as it exploded against the wall.

Juliet felt all the trauma she had suffered recently boil up inside her, anger the likes of which she had never experienced. She'd lost her boyfriend, her dad was missing, she thought she had lost her babies, and now someone was trying to kill her.

Beside her was a five-foot standard lamp with a brass neck. She tore it from the socket and screamed her frustration at the woman.

She met her head-on, holding the lamp in both hands like a kali staff.

The courier slashed with the knife and Juliet caught her beneath the chin with the lampshade.

She heard the crunch of the light-bulb as the thing connected and dodged another one of the woman's attacks.

The woman struck out with the blade again.

Juliet raised the lamp in time to deflect her arm's trajectory; she twisted it around and thrust the heavy solid base towards the woman's chest. The woman fell over the arm of the sofa and onto the cushions and Juliet wasted no time in jumping on top of her. She wedged the brass neck beneath her chin and pushed with all her weight.

The woman dropped her knife and fought to get the lamp off her throat.

Juliet pressed harder, lessening the pressure only when the courier's arms began to weaken. "Why?" Juliet screamed. "Tell me why."

The woman struggled to speak so Juliet relaxed the pressure some more. "They're going to kill your children."

Juliet felt herself go weak.

The woman instantly reached for the knife.

FERAL

"No," Juliet roared and thrust the metal against the woman's throat once more. She felt something inside the woman's neck give, her oesophagus crushing, and her eyes bugged as she fought for breath.

Juliet recoiled and ran to the other side of the room as the woman clawed at her throat and her face went purple, capillaries bursting in the whites of her eyes.

"Sorry, sorry, sorry." All Juliet could do was cry as the courier lost consciousness.

*

Charlotte couldn't believe they were actually going to take the kids to McDonald's.

The driver introduced himself as Davis, no 'Mister,' or, as she was expecting, 'Agent.' The other men were Spencer, Simon, and Fry.

Davis stopped the van and was out of the vehicle switching his phone on. He had his back to her but she saw his face reflected in the restaurant windows. He seemed to be just listening.

She tried her door, but it was locked. "Hey, can I get out and get my phone?" she asked the man to her right.

"Best wait until Davis gets back in."

Charlotte sighed. "So, is he your boss?"

"Yeah, something like that."

"Which one are you? He fired names off left, right, and centre but I didn't match them up with bods."

"Fry," the man said, and smiled somewhat awkwardly.

"Is your first name French?" Kiran blurted out, causing Kayleigh to squeal with mirth.

Fry blushed and faked laughter.

In the half-light, Charlotte saw a constellation of freckles, spread across his face and shaved scalp. "Don't be rude, kids."

"It's fine," Fry said. "Imagine if my first name were Pierre and I came from Paris. Then I really would be a French fry."

Charlotte smiled at his cringeworthy attempt at humour, which in turn made his cheeks redden more. Her mind returned to her phone and Juliet'sapparent crisis. "I need some fresh air."

She squeezed through to the front seats before any of the men could object.

Davis was startled when he saw her behind the steering wheel. He put his phone away and yanked open the door. "What the hell are you playing at?"

"Sorry," Charlotte said, with a crooked grin that she knew some men found cute, "I just need to get out and stretch my legs." She scooted beneath his arm. "And talk to you."

"Your little problem has been solved," he said, leading her away from the van.

"You've heard from her?"

Davis nodded. "My contacts are with her now. Everything is fine."

"But you never spoke to Juliet herself?"

"No, but everything is in safe hands."

Charlotte didn't believe him. "Mind if I have my phone back now?"

"Of course." He handed her the phone without hesitation.

She switched it on as he moved back to the van. "What are you doing?"

"Getting the children's orders."

"Yeah, we can hardly have two little kids and their armed escort going inside for a Happy Meal," she said, half-joking.

"Who says we're armed?"

"Oh, you're armed. I know it." Her phone came to life and she immediately dialled Juliet'snumber.

"It's gone to voicemail."

"Doctor Charlotte," Davis began softly, "their mother is safe. One of the local thugs tried to mug her, but believe me, they ended up a lot worse than she did."

Charlotte held his gaze. It sounded plausible, and fighter or not, Juliet was no shrinking violet; she had no doubt the woman could stick up for herself. She wasn't going to be satisfied until she spoke to her in person, but as there was nothing else she could do, she continued with the matter at hand. "Come on. I want a fillet of fish; two, if you guys are paying."

Chapter 27

Mortimer was bored. The only thing they were doing at the facility was observation. Of course, he didn't want to be experimented on, like he did with the old man, but it was what he expected. It was worrying that Butcher's people knew enough about lycanthropy not to need to dissect him; they even had procedures on what to do when he was ready for his first transformation.

It meant he might not be as valuable as he'd once thought. That he might be expendable. He needed to prove himself worthy, which is what Butcher had implied, but how?

He needed to know what was going on, what Butcher's contacts were planning.

The portly Ukrainian seemed just as bored. He sat with his feet up on his desk, doing a crossword.

"What's going on, Gustav?"

Gustav moved the pen he was chewing from one side of his mouth to the other. "Not much."

"With Butcher, I meant."

"Pah." Gustav thrust the pen towards him, sending a strand of spittle his way. "They don't tell me anything other than we are having two more of your kind coming, and to prepare."

Mortimer remembered Butcher mentioning the arrival of twins. "How come they've known about this since the forties?"

Gustav shrugged. "There's a lot of things that get covered up. Not everything the tinfoil hat warriors say is wrong." He tapped his temples. "We are told what to believe."

"But werewolves? Surely if this sort of thing has been known about for so long, we would have heard about it?"

"And who would have believed it, eh?" Gustav flapped a hand at him. "This? This is nothing." He leant forward in his chair, his belly hanging between his knees and threatening to propel shirt buttons. "Do you know the *real* reason for the Chernobyl disaster?"

"What?"

Gustav smiled triumphantly. "I do. I was part of the cover-up." He paused to build up Mortimer's anticipation. "Extra-terrestrial contamination."

"Like hell!"

"It's true," he said, slamming his pen down. "Something alien landed and targeted the reactor. It's probably still there beneath the concrete."

Mortimer scoffed; it was hard to take the man seriously.

Gustav swatted at him with his newspaper. "And yet here you are, a thing of legend. A living, breathing werewolf."

"But eventually," Mortimer said with a sigh, "science will explain this."

"There are some things that can't be explained, no matter how much you pull them apart."

Mortimer shook his head. "Everything has a scientific explanation."

Gustav laughed and unfolded his newspaper. "You are the sheep. Baa, baa. Just you wait until I tell you what's been happening in Antarctica for the last hundred or so years."

"I can't believe they trained *you* in cryogenics," Mortimer snorted as Gustav went through the details of the imminent procedure.

Gustav tapped a finger against his temple. "My mind. It is like a sponge."

"What if it goes wrong?"

Gustav sneered. "It won't go wrong. You think, maybe, I haven't done this before? That I'm just a trainee? Let me tell you, Doctor, we are much more advanced in these procedures than we let the world know. Did you know that already there have been ten people reawakened from cryogenic sleep?"

"No, of course I didn't." What Mortimer would have found preposterous before didn't surprise him at all now.

"We defrosted Walt Disney in 2009; he still runs his company."

Mortimer laughed; it was hard to tell whether or not he was joking.

"It's true. You would be amazed at what can be done but is kept quiet. Death and disease are just tiny obstacles if the money is right."

"So, why hasn't Butcher managed to cure whatever it is that ails him?"

Gustav scratched his moustache. "Why do you think?"

Mortimer had his suspicions. "Either he can't, or he's waiting for something specific. He spoke of someone else, in Germany, someone superior to him. Is that it? Is he waiting for permission?" Then realisation dawned on him. "He's going to infect himself with lycanthropy, isn't he?"

Gustav raised his hands. "I have said nothing."

"He's waiting to perfect this lunacy, isn't he? Waiting until they know everything about it, how to control it, and then he'll infect himself."

Gustav eyed the CCTV camera in the corner of the room and shrugged.

"What's this all for, Gustav?" Mortimer slumped against his restraints. "What's the point in all this? I can understand the healing properties but I don't believe that's all they're interested in. They're going to sell it to the military, aren't they?"

"My job is not to ask questions." Gustav unhooked a bag on one of the drips which surrounded Mortimer. "This will be your last fluid intake until after the process."

"Look, isn't there some other way to do this?" Mortimer whined. "If a group of OAPs can do it without all this hi-tech malarkey, then why can't I?"

"Perhaps you can, perhaps you can't. This way is certain. You can hardly change into a wolf if you're clinically dead."

"Come again? I thought I was just going into cryosleep?"

Gustav chuckled. "Whilst our technology is far more advanced than the world knows, unfortunately we cannot perform such miracles; maybe in a year or two. Tomorrow evening, just before your predicted transformation time, you will be injected with pentobarbital, which will render you unconscious quite swiftly. Then an injection of pancuronium bromide, which will cause complete paralysis, and finally potassium chloride to stop your heart."

Mortimer paled. "You're going to give me the lethal fucking injection."

"Relax," Gustav said with a nonchalant wave of his hand.

"Don't tell me to relax. What if it goes wrong?"

Gustav shrugged again. "Then we will replace your blood with a special solution. This will preserve your organs and stop your fluids from freezing when you go into the liquid nitrogen."

"You can't let them do this to me, Gustav. It's barbaric."

"But not when it was you experimenting on the old man, eh? If Germany had known about this, and you hadn't let him escape, then perhaps he could have been the guinea pig—"

"Wait," Mortimer spluttered. "You mean this hasn't been done before?"

"It will be the first time it is performed in England, yes."

Mortimer was numb. They were going to kill him and rely on the lycanthropy for resuscitation. There were questions upon questions—upon questions.

If they removed all of his bodily fluids, how would the lycanthropy work?

Would they thaw him out and stick his blood back in and hope for the best, or did they know more than they were letting on about this thing?

"They know, don't they? The people in Germany."

"I do not follow."

"They know where the lycanthropy hides inside the body."

It was obvious they wouldn't be resorting to measures like this if they didn't fully understand the monstrous thing.

"Is it in the brain? It is, isn't it? Like mutated cordyceps?"

Once more, Gustav eyed the camera in the corner but this time the blood drained from his face. "No comment."

FERAL

Chapter 28
1945

They had been looking for Krauss since the soldier who had accompanied him to his execution returned to camp with a broken nose.

When Liebermann heard about the empty grave, he knew straight away what the doctor had done. As much as he hated the man for his betrayal to the fatherland, he admired his cunning, and now there was hope again.

After his meagre experiments were destroyed in the bombing he really had been close to putting his Mauser in his mouth and pulling the trigger. But this, *this* was good news. The lycanthropy was still out there.

How hard could it be to find a pair of geriatrics? He would scour the land until he found them. There was no way they would leave the country.

It was as though she'd crawled out of a death pit naked and shivering. The only thing covering Gwen was the compacted filth she had accumulated over the weeks since her burial. Her hair was a matted nest of dried blood and dirt.

There was nothing behind her eyes; no life, no spark of recognition.

Victor's gut wound made him double over despite the rapid healing.

She seemed to notice him, at last, maybe because he was in pain. "What have you done to yourself?"

Victor laughed at her forthright tone, making the pain a whole lot worse. "Oh, I've been clumsy."

FERAL

Gwen nodded and went back to staring into space. Her dementia was worse than ever.

Victor hoped the wolfblood would have stopped — or slowed — its course, miraculous as the stuff was. But it didn't matter. They had found one another and that was the main thing.

The hard part would be getting her out of the country.

He took Gwen's arm and noticed her strength. "Come on, we need to make ourselves presentable before we get to Offenburg."

They staggered through the forest like antiquated, stop-motion zombies.

Victor didn't want to hurt anyone else.

The farmer and farmhand were more than enough, especially considering he had torn their heads from their corpses to prevent any chances of the virus spreading.

But he knew he would do whatever he had to for he and Gwen to survive.

It wasn't long before the forest cleared and they came to the first house.

A woman stood pegging washing on a line. When she saw them come from the trees, she clutched at her chest as though she was about to keel over.

"Hilde, Hilde," she shrieked, and from the house came a younger woman, sharing her likeness: her daughter.

They stared, a mixture of fear and revulsion, but as Victor and Gwen stepped into the daylight and the women saw how old and decrepit they were, their fear turned to pity and they went to their aid.

Hilde and her mother helped them into the small house where Victor gave them an edited version of the truth.

They had been beaten and left for dead by the SS. There was nothing else he could think of saying that would justify their appearance, and it wasn't far removed from actual events. The women weren't as gullible as he thought, but they asked no questions as they tended to the couple's wounds.

"My husband did not want to fight in this war," the mother said, as she sponged the debris out of Victor's injuries.

The shotgun pellets had worked their way out of his body before they'd left the forest; now it was just a raw, grazed area surrounded by purple bruising.

"What is your name?" Victor asked. He estimated the lady to be in her fifties; her hair was showing the beginnings of grey.

"Hannalore," she said quietly.

"Oh, how lovely," Victor said. "It's Hebrew, I believe?"

The woman stopped what she was doing and pursed her lips. "I know what it is you are thinking, and yes, you are right. We are Jews."

Victor took her hand. "Madam, I hold no prejudice against any race or colour, only the sadistic bastards who are running this country and murdering innocent people. So many innocent people."

Hannalore nodded.

"Your husband is safer in the army than he would be in the camp. There are many Jews fighting in this war. The world knows no one has much choice in whether they fight or not. I hope he comes back to you."

"Thank you," Hannalore said, and finished washing his stomach.

Hilde came in, quiet as a mouse. "Mother, there is clean water and clothing."

"Of course." Hannalore stood, adjusted her pinafore, and helped Victor to his feet. "If you come this way, you may be with your wife. Hilde has some clothes that should fit you."

Victor finished cleaning himself and Gwen up, horrified by how emaciated they were. What was he thinking?

What he had done was an abomination.

His plans of killing himself and his wife resurfaced now they were reunited.

Even if Gwen was in charge of her faculties, with a mind as fresh as his it would still be wrong to prolong lives in bodies as decrepit as these.

What good was immortality, or at least an extended existence, if trapped in such a weathered vessel?

The only reason he had infected them both was so they could escape Nazi Germany and die in peace in the country of their choosing. This was only meant to be temporary, and so it would be.

Hilde drove them into Offenburg, the road pockmarked and ruined.

Civilisation brought the first people Victor had seen in weeks, at least in groups.

He wondered what Gwen had done during that time.

Had the thing within left her to rot, aside from when it was time to feed?

She carried herself better.

The wolf had certainly repaired some of her physical ailments, making its host the best vessel possible.

Schäfer had said that if you couldn't control the wolf during your first transformation, it would always have the upper hand. Every full moon, it would surface whether you liked it or not, and feed continuously.

He desperately wanted to know more about lycanthropy and how it worked.

If he concentrated enough, he could sense the virus inside him, like a semi-sentient thing, another personality. As a doctor, his thirst for knowledge constantly tried to override what he knew he must do eventually.

In a matter of days, by his rough judgement, the moon would be full again — and his wife uncontrollable.

She needed to be somewhere safe by then.

Somewhere safe. Or dead.

Offenburg swarmed with life, the train station overrun with German soldiers. Vampiric SS commanders strode through the hordes, swathed in black. Soldiers stopped people at random to check their papers and passports.

Victor said farewell to Hilde and took Gwen's arm and crossed the station foyer.

He hadn't been to the station since the early days of the conflict, when he'd wanted to plant one of his back-up caches.

They were supposed to have been retired.

He cursed Liebermann and the Nazis for delving into this absurdity.

It shouldn't have surprised him; the Nazi Party had its roots in the occult; he recognised their doctored runes and symbols for what they originally were.

Every day he worked for them, he would hang his head in shame. He loved his country but hated how it was bewitched by a racist madman.

A member of the Schutzstaffel locked eyes on him through the crowd, and he gripped Gwen more tightly. "Come on, we need to hurry."

Schutzstaffel meant Protection Squad, which he found ironic considering they were some of the vilest men in the country.

The SS commander, along with several soldiers, moved across the station, elbowing passers-by out of their path.

Victor pulled Gwen towards the left luggage area, hoping and praying that the locker he had hired would still be there.

The soldiers closed in, the man in black shouting something incoherent.

"Oh, thank God." He spotted the left luggage room, where he could see the lockers through the open door. He quickened his pace. Gwen began to struggle; his panicking had made her anxious.

"Please, Gwen. We need to be quick."

"Will we miss the train?"

"Yes." Victor heard screams and saw the commander with a gun in his hand. People scattered. He needed to be able to get to the locker and retrieve his things before they saw him.

Knowing exactly what he was risking, he ushered his wife to a nearby bench and told her to wait for him.

Gwen did as she was asked, and he slipped into the room.

He rushed to find the correct numbered locker; each compartment was fastened with a combination lock.

There was always going to be a chance they were robbed, or the lockers removed, so it was a welcome sight when he found the right one.

He twisted the lock's digits to the date of their wedding and pocketed the bundle within. When he came out of the room, he saw Gwen surrounded by the soldiers and the SS commander.

FERAL

Chapter 29

Charlotte got back in the van with the twins, who babbled their orders at Davis, who in turn, sent two of his men to get the food.

"We make less of a scene this way," he said, turning and winking at them. Much to Charlotte 's horror, she was beginning to like the man.

Fry moved into the passenger seat beside Davis and politely asked Charlotte and the kids to excuse them. He pressed a switch on the dashboard and a black partition slid down to separate the front and rear.

Charlotte seized the opportunity to use her phone again; to hell with what they said, the vehicle wasn't moving.

She was surprised when Juliet's number connected.

*

Panic rose and threatened to consume her. If it did, it would be over.

Even though Juliet was in the presence of two murdered people, her immediate concern was her children.

What the hell had the courier meant?

Who the bloody hell was she?

Who was trying to kill them?

And why?

It wasn't some random attack; the courier had known Juliet had kids.

She was full of unanswered questions.

Music started playing and it took a few seconds for her to realise it was her ringtone. When she was attacked, the same number had called her: it was the doctor, her children's doctor.

Her phone was wedged between the sofa and the dead woman's hip. She grabbed it, pressed answer, and jammed it against her ear. "Hello?"

"Hey, it's Doctor Smith—"

"Are my babies okay?"

"Yeah, they're fine, we're at the Sudbury drive-thru McDonald's. It's you I wanted to check on. You said someone was…umm…bothering you when I rang earlier."

Something was wrong.

"Why are my children at McDonald's?"

"Oh," Doctor Smith said, startled. "We're on the way to the facility and the guys who are escorting us made a stop-off." She gave a nervous laugh. "I didn't think it would be a problem, you said they didn't have any dietary requirements. I can al—"

"Please, Doctor, I don't know what's going on. What facility? I don't know anything about a facility!" The tears she had tried so desperately to hold back now came in floods. "A woman tried to kill me. She told me my kids were going to be killed. Please don't hurt my babies, I'll do anything."

The doctor began to speak but was cut off by a man's voice and the sounds of shouting and a struggle.

Juliet heard her daughter's brief scream and then the call ended.

*

"What the hell do you think you are doing?" Charlotte cried over the twins' sudden outburst.

Spencer threw a paper sack of fast food at her and retrieved her phone from the footwell. Simon was behind him with a tray full of drinks, which he dropped to the van roof.

The front doors slammed and Davis and Fry joined them.

Spencer handed Davis Charlotte's phone. "She was talking to the kids' mother."

"For fuck's sake," Davis snapped, colour rising in his cheeks. "Restrain her and shut the kids up, we're leaving. We should never have stopped."

Charlotte screamed and lashed out with everything she had at Spencer and Simon.

Kiran shook and screamed; Kayleigh was rigid with terror and confusion.

"Help," Charlotte managed, when she spotted people leaving the restaurant, three men laden down with food.

They stared at the scene, half-stunned, half-suspicious, before one of them dropped his food and charged towards them. His friends followed suit.

"Now look what you've made us do," Davis said coolly, and nodded to Fry, who whipped out a pistol from inside his jacket. A slight whistle came from the silenced gun and the closest man fell to the tarmac. His two friends stumbled over their fallen comrade and saw the hole in his head and the brains spread across the carpark. They didn't have enough time to say anything; Fry dispatched them similarly within seconds.

"We need to leave now," Davis said.

Simon and Spencer dove into the rear of the van and Fry got into the front.

The van pulled away; Charlotte still kicked out at the two men but it was pointless. Simon caught her flailing wrists and brought them together as Spencer slipped what looked like a metal zip tie over them, the wire biting through her flesh. She saw the abstract fear on the children's faces. "I'm so sorry. I don't know what's happening."

Spencer pinned her legs down and wrapped another loop around her ankles. "You're lucky we don't do anything else," he said. As she opened her mouth to protest he grabbed hold of one of her breasts and stared at her in such a way it shut her up immediately.

*

Her mind was in turmoil.

Should she go to the police?

The hospital?

Juliet stared at her phone; every paranoid conspiracy theory and spy film she had ever seen went through her head.

They knew what she looked like, where she lived, probably everything about her.

Maybe her phone was being tracked.

She wanted to know who they were and whether the courier was only the first of many.

They wanted her children.

Something in their blood, something new.

Kiran's appendix had regenerated.

Everything pointed to the rumours surrounding Boxford.

If there really were werewolves tearing around the country, the government would try to cover it up.

All that mattered to Juliet was finding her babies. She needed to know where they were.

Juliet stared into space as she figured out what to do next. "Where are they? Where are they?" she whispered to herself repeatedly. Something clicked inside her, and she stood determined and defiant.

The courier's knife was still covered in Peter's blood. She picked it up and cleaned it on his curtains.

She had never seen anything like it before. It was a solid ten-inch black Maglite with a six-inch blade protruding from the handle. When she twisted the neck of the torch, a powerful beam almost blinded her. A button on it sucked the knife back into the handle. It was a deadly inventive tool, like a James Bond gadget. She took the weapon and left Peter's flat, determined to find her children — whatever the cost.

FERAL

Part Three

FERAL

Chapter 30

"Oh, Jesus fuck." Tony hung his head.

"Who. The. Fuck. Is Cyril?" Danny asked again.

"A client," Tony murmured.

Danny dropped the paper on the table and sighed. "I still can't get used to this other side of you. It's as sleazy as fuck. I mean, you being gay was fine, but…"

Tony felt shame wash over him and channelled it into anger. "I did it as a way out. Out of that shitty town, that shitty fucking life. I never knew half the stuff you were getting up to with the GMC."

"Yeah, but I wasn't doing stuff like this."

"Oh, and mugging old people is better? Look, I'm not proud of it. I just wanted to get gone."

"What about me?"

Danny sounded the same as he had back when they were kids and he was about to cry. Tony saw the hurt in his eyes; he felt the same. "Our relationship wasn't exactly what I'd call close before this kicked off."

"But we're brothers!"

"No, the GMC were your brothers. Are you telling me that you wouldn't have put Neep and his cronies before me? If it had come down to it?" Tony regretted his words as soon as they'd come out, but it was true; he could tell by the look on Danny's face. He held his brother's arm to try and prevent him from running off in a sulk and was alarmed by the strength he felt.

Danny snatched his arm away but didn't storm off. Was he growing up, or was it because there was no safe place to run to? "Things would have been different if Mum was still alive."

Tony couldn't argue with that; she had definitely ruled the roost. "We were so young when she died I'm surprised you can remember her."

Again, Danny looked hurt. "Course I do. I remember her singing all the time. I remember Christmases being something to look forward to; not just for presents, but for us all piling under the duvet to watch films and eat crap. I remember Dad being happy, everywhere being clean."

Tony remembered their dad coming home from the pub every night and beating the crap out of her for cheating on him when she rarely left the flat other than to go shopping.

He wondered what she would think of them now. "Look, we've got each other now, that's all that matters, and I promise I'll never leave you. Okay?"

Danny nodded and wiped a tear from his cheek. "You can't see that Cyril bloke. Cancel him. Tell him you've got the shits or something. Whatever happens tomorrow, we face it full on, deal with it, and take your man's stash and split."

"Okay."

"That's it? No arguments?"

"No. You're right. I've had enough of this shit. I don't want to be used by vile old men anymore. No amount of money will wipe the shit I've done from my head. Let's do this." Tony took the cheap mobile phone and began typing in numbers.

"What are you doing?"

"Cancelling Cyril."

*

Cyril stabbed a finger at the dashboard, pressed a button to end the call, and screamed.

He slowed the car, spun the steering wheel, and performed an illegal U-turn across of two lanes of busy traffic.

Drivers braked, tyres squealed, and angry faces shouted through windows.

"Here we have an improvised symphony from the horn section." Cyril laughed like a madman at the cacophony he had created.

He moved up a gear and weaved around a double decker bus.

He upped the volume of his music, and The Bee Gees screamed about getting a message to you, louder than the makeshift orchestra outside.

Cyril's car shot up the road towards the hospital like a blob of mustard fired from a peashooter.

He could hear the poncey bastard's voice echo through the ward, almost every sentence ending with that annoying *ha-ha* of his.

When he had last spoken to him, after the stroke, he had lost his usual eloquence, but it was back in full force now.

He strode past the small reception towards Bartholomew's voice.

Bartholomew was propped up on several pillows, his grey hair draped over tartan pyjamas, deep in conversation with a couple of nurses.

He could charm anyone if he set his mind to it, though the moment he saw Cyril, his whole demeanour changed.

His face fell, the drooping on the one side betraying the weakness there.

FERAL

"Excuse me, ladies. It appears I have a surprise visitor, ha-ha."

The nurses' first fleeting reactions of seeing Cyril were amusement and mild disgust.

Cyril loitered awkwardly in the middle of the ward, avoiding eye contact.

He knew Bartholomew wouldn't be happy; he loathed impromptu visits as much as he did.

The nurses walked past him and he waited for the secretive shared laughter that almost always followed when people saw him for the first time. It came and he dug his fingernails into his palms and rolled his eyes towards the ceiling.

"Come," Bartholomew summoned from the bed. "Sit down where you're not so much on show, ha-ha."

Cyril's loafers squeaked as he crossed the floor; an elderly man doing a crossword eyed him over his bifocals.

Cyril sat on a green armchair, his trousers riding up mid-shin. "Should I draw the curtains?"

"Oh God, no." Bartholomew laughed. "It's not like you're here to give me a bloody bed bath, is it?"

Cyril could tell he was annoyed despite his outwardly jovial manner.

"Just remember where you are and mind your Ps and Qs." Bartholomew nodded to the old men occupying three of the other five beds. "Gerald and Winston over there are sound as houses, and Harry here is as deaf as a post." He raised a hand to the man filling out his puzzle book. "Aren't you, Harry?"

Harry gave him a thumbs-up.

"Deaf old cunt," Bartholomew muttered under his breath, then turned towards Cyril, his dark eyes boring into him.

Cyril knew better than to avoid eye contact with Bartholomew.

Under the man's glare, his eyes were alive with all manner of uncontrollable tics, rapid blinking, rolling, unable to settle in their sockets, but always being drawn back to Bartholomew's obsidian pools.

"So, why the unexpected visit?"

Even though Bartholomew was sure no one could hear them, Cyril was taking no chances. He leaned closer. "Tony cancelled my visit. Reckons he's ill."

"Fuck." A darkness swept over his face.

"I've been keeping an eye on things, like you asked."

"Fucking little pricks," Bartholomew spat, releasing a line of drool from the corner of his mouth. A vein, tree-like, bulged in his forehead.

"Don't get yourself worked up, not in the state you're in."

Bartholomew closed his eyes and tried to calm himself down.

Cyril could see his body lolling to one side. "Want me to get the nurse?"

Bartholomew shook his head. "Relax, I'm not about to keel over again just yet. I'm almost back to normal, they say. Just a little weak."

"Okay. What do you want me to do?"

"Go to the workhouse, break in if you have to. Make sure they're still there and that they are not hiding anything."

"Hiding anything? Like what?"

Bartholomew opened his eyes and locked him in his glare. "Three briefcases full of incriminating items."

Cyril's eyes quit their nervous roaming and froze.

"I know they've tampered with them. I know they're on the run. There's enough in those cases for them to disappear but also enough to finish me off."

Cyril was speechless.

"If I go down, you're coming with me, Cyril," Bartholomew whispered.

His weakened hand rested on Cyril's forearm and attempted to squeeze. "I know all about Samuel Ellington, I know all about what you get up to amongst the flowers in Bluebell Wood."

Cyril gulped so severely he began choking on his own saliva. He slammed against the chair, loud enough to rouse the deaf man from his crossword.

Bartholomew pointed at the jug of water on the bedside cabinet. "Oh, do stop making a scene."

As Cyril fumbled with the jug and a plastic beaker, Bartholomew turned to Harry and raised his voice. "I think he wants to be in here getting the special treatment with us, Harry. Probably fancies the nurses, ha-ha."

Harry grinned and nodded.

"You have no idea what I'm saying, do you?" Bartholomew said, grinning with gritted teeth.

Cyril brought his coughing under control, beads of sweat dotting his bald head.

"Relax," Bartholomew said. "I told you years ago I don't care what extracurricular activities you get up to, as long as they don't involve me."

Cyril couldn't help but snort. "But you're involving me."

Bartholomew took a deep breath and let it out slowly. "You've always been a trustworthy acquaintance, and yes, you're right, I am involving you." He gripped Cyril's wrist again, more firmly this time. "I need your help. Which is why I'm rewarding you."

"Rewarding me?"

"Go to the house," Bartholomew whispered. "If the boys are there, do what the hell you like to them. Just make sure they don't leave in a healthy enough condition to tell anyone what they saw in those cases."

FERAL

Chapter 31
1945

Victor approached Gwen and the soldiers with all the speed and frailty that one would expect from a man of his age.

Fortunately, he didn't recognise any of the men — and he was good at remembering faces.

As he got closer he forced a smile and adjusted his coat. "Ah, the moment I turn my back, you are entertaining the troops."

They remained stony-faced.

"Did you not hear us calling you?" the SS commander sneered beneath his black cap.

Victor waved a hand at the crowds. "There is such a lot of commotion, sir. I heard something but my eyesight isn't so good. I foolishly assumed it would be no business of two elderly folk. I apologise profusely."

"Are you travelling?"

Victor nodded. "We are at a train station, no? Yes, sir, we hope to go to Zurich."

"Do you have your documentation?"

"Yes, sir, I do. It would be hard to leave the country without it."

The commander held out a black-gloved hand. Victor's natural hesitance made him draw his pistol.

"Please," Victor begged, "there is no need for that. My wife is ill."

The weapon was lowered.

Victor slid a hand inside his jacket and took out his and Gwen's passports.

The commander flipped open the first and looked up at him. "Bernard Muller."

"At your service." Victor bowed.

"Born 17th of September 1862?"

"No, sir. That says 12th."

The passport was handed to a soldier whilst the other was examined.

The commander scrutinised Gwen's photo before addressing her. "And your name?"

Victor made to answer but the commander glared at him and raised his gun.

This is where it goes wrong, Victor thought, as he took in Gwen's empty expression.

A black-gloved hand waved in front of her face; the thumb and forefingers clicked when she gave no response.

"Please," Victor said, "she has moments like this where she is almost catatonic. I can answer any questions you need to ask."

"I'm sure you can," the commander said suspiciously. He took the other passport from the soldier and addressed the others. "I'm going to make a phone call. Don't let them leave."

It took every ounce of self-control Victor had not to let fear show on his face.

He could sense the thing inside him reacting to his emotions, begging to be let out, to rise and rip them apart.

The crowds parted like the sea for Moses.

Victor could feel the SS commander's eyes on him as he came across the concourse. If they were going to be captured, this was the time. There was no way Victor would risk anything in front of all these innocent bystanders. He hoped Gwen would remain in her fugue state, impassive as ever. If her monster detected a threat, carnage would follow. There were children here, families, the elderly; her wolf wouldn't discriminate when it came to tearing people apart.

Victor stepped forward, up to the ring of soldiers guarding them, away from Gwen. "Please, sir," he said, keeping up the polite old man act, "if there is a problem, please let's not argue in front of my wife."

The fleeting smile gracing the commander's face was an alien thing. With the same hand that only moments before had pointed a pistol, he passed Victor the passports back. "No problem, Herr Muller. I wish you and your wife a safe journey."

Victor took the passports warily, waiting for the catch that would surely present itself, but it never came.

The commander led the group of soldiers away across the forecourt, to continue their random spot-checks of documents and identification. Victor hoped they really were just exercising their power, performing routine inspections, but his feeling of unease remained as he escorted Gwen to the ticket office.

After he had waited in the queue, and subsequently purchased a pair of one-way tickets to Budapest, he noticed the soldiers had gone.

He surveyed the arrivals and departures board and located the platform for their train.

The journey would take twelve hours, crossing Germany, Austria, and halfway along the Hungarian border.

He was taking Gwen back to her favourite place on Earth, where they had become engaged.

He didn't know how he was going to do it, but once they had stood on the Széchenyi Chain Bridge, he would end their lives and put a stop to lycanthropy.

Chapter 32

Cyril shook with excitement.

By the time night fell, he had checked the boot of his car half a dozen times.

He was empowered, an assassin about to carry out a hit.

He would do what Bartholomew said and reap the rewards afterwards...*and during*.

His driving was erratic.

He was determined to arrive at the time of his allocated — and subsequently cancelled — appointment.

There was a paper bag from the pharmacy on the passenger seat, filled with anti-sickness and anti-diarrhoea medication.

He would tell them Bartholomew had sent him to help, tell them he knew they were in hiding, and take from there.

He had a slight worry that the brothers would have left already, absconded with Bartholomew's loot. If that was the case, then that was the way it was meant to be.

What happens happens.

Oh, how he hated that phrase. He liked to think he was in control of his own destiny.

He always had trouble when things didn't go his way.

He parked the car outside the boarded-up houses without caring that someone might see such a distinctive coloured vehicle.

It didn't matter.

He had no plans on using it after the night was over.

FERAL

He went over it meticulously to remove anything he needed.

By the end of the night, it would light up Bluebell Wood, and tomorrow he would report it stolen.

He grabbed the bag of drugs and wandered along the desolate street. The council would knock the lot down once the one or two stubborn residents at the far end had kicked the bucket. No one had lived down this end for at least five years.

He stepped over a crumbled garden wall and waded through overgrown grass as though he was the hero in some post-apocalyptic saga, the last man alive.

*

Tony switched off the boiling kettle in case it could be heard from outside.

"Don't answer it," Danny said, following Tony into the kitchen.

The knocking on the door became more rapid.

Someone called out for Tony.

"Oh, fucking hell, it's Cyril."

"You cancelled him," Danny said. "Why is he here?"

"How the hell should I know? He's a sad old wanker who has formed some kind of emotional attachment to me. He probably wants to check if I'm alright."

Danny relaxed a little and then brightened up. "Tell him to go and get us KFC."

"Are you taking the piss?"

Danny smirked. "Maybe a bit, but if he's as obsessed with you as you think, he might do it."

"No," Tony whispered, "he'll expect something in return." He frowned. "Look, he's relatively harmless, a nervous weirdo, shakes all the time. I'll let him in and get rid of him ASAP. Don't want him attracting anyone else here."

"I'm not going anywhere. If he tries owt, I'll kick his arse."

"Sure thing." Tony unfastened the locks and bolts and opened the door.

Cyril loomed over the threshold ghoulish and tall; no doorway seemed tall enough to enable him passage without ducking.

"Hello, Tony," he said, breathless. "I brought you some medicine." He held up a brown paper bag and a four-pack of supermarket brand cola.

"Oh, wow, that's very thoughtful of you," Tony began.

"I'd better come in, there was a police car doing the rounds a few minutes back." Cyril squeezed past him then spotted Danny. "Is this your little brother?"

Tony closed the door but hesitated when it came to locking it. "Who told you he was my brother?"

Cyril stammered and stuttered while he desperately tried to think of an answer.

"Fuck's sake," Tony said, gently headbutting the door.

"What's the matter?" Danny asked, giving Cyril a wary side glance.

"Tepes has told him we're here."

"Hey," Cyril said, eyes twitching, hands shaking. "It's cool. I'm cool. I ain't going to say anything. Me and Bartholomew go back years."

Tony nodded and fought back anger.

There was nothing he could do other than keep the creepy bastard sweet. "I'm sorry I had to cancel you tonight."

Danny glared at him in disgust.

"I don't know what it is," Tony continued, ignoring his brother's expression. "Maybe it's all these instant noodles Bartholomew left us, I'm used to my five-a-day, you know?"

Cyril nodded. "If you want I can go and get you boys some shopping?"

Danny stuck his thumbs up behind Cyril and mouthed, "KFC."

"I don't know, Cyril. We've not got any money."

"I'll get it, no bother." His eyes rested on Tony's face, his grey tongue wet his lips. "You can owe me."

That was exactly what Tony was worried about, what he would want in return, but then he thought about Tepes' cases and hoped they would be far away by the time it came to paying Cyril back. "Okay, that would be brilliant. Thank you."

"Yeah," Danny piped up, "thanks, dude. And if you happen to go past a KFC on your wa—"

"Danny!" Tony spluttered.

Cyril laughed.

"Chill out, lads. I've got your backs." He awkwardly thumped his chest like he'd seen some kids do in town. His eyes lingered on Danny. "I'll get you the biggest bucket they do."

Tony thought about what Danny had said, his brother was right. Of all the seedy things he had done to this man for money, nowhere near *enough* money, it was high time he used him back. "You're a star, Cyril, I'll make a list of what we need."

"Sure thing," he said.

He put the medication on a worktop and opened the pack of cola. "Mind if I have a drink first?"

"No, course not, mate." Tony shrugged.

Cyril handed them a can each and cracked his. "Cheers."

Danny opened his and guzzled it like an alcoholic with their first drink of the day.

Tony brought his can towards his lips and saw minute bubbles popping out of a tiny perforation. Something had pierced the aluminium. "Danny, stop."

Danny looked at the can. "Mine's alright, they probably got knocked around."

"Yeah," Tony said, unsure, but when he locked eyes on Cyril he knew something was wrong. "Cyril, what did you—" was all he managed to get out as Cyril swiped the kettle from the counter and smashed it into his face.

FERAL

Chapter 33

After the men had made themselves clear just how important their mission was, Charlotte kept quiet. The man, Spencer, had groped her in front of the other men and not one of them had berated him for it —and those poor men who had tried to help her had been shot without hesitation.

Her parents had brought her up to be tougher than this, and she hated how useless she felt. Charlotte fought the fear inside, refusing to let it overwhelm her.

The kids were hysterical when everything kicked off, but several miles down the road, a stern determination far beyond her years took over Kayleigh.

"We're here." It was the first thing Davis had said since they'd left the fast-food restaurant.

Charlotte saw them pass a sign for an army barracks she had never heard of, and they drove towards a small checkpoint.

Two soldiers, armed with heavy-looking automatic guns, stood before a high, razor-topped fence.

After exchanging a few words with Davis, one of the soldiers signalled for the gates to be opened, and a large section of the fence slid across.

"What is this place?" Charlotte asked.

Spencer smirked at the fear on her face. "If you're kept alive long enough, I'm sure you'll find out."

"Why are we here?" Kayleigh snapped.

"I want my mum." Kiran sniffed back tears.

Spencer laughed at them. "Welcome to your new home, kids."

"Shut the fuck up, Spencer," Davis said, turning towards them.

All Charlotte could think of were his words about being kept alive long enough.

What the hell was going on with these kids?

Through the front window she saw army jeeps criss-crossing over a wide expanse that was clearly an airfield, judging by the Chinook helicopter that slowly lowered to the asphalt, drowning out all other sound.

They drew close to a floodlit building.

People waited, soldiers, and there was something that resembled a futuristic golf cart. When it stopped beneath a floodlight, she saw it was an electric wheelchair, holding a small, withered figure. "Who the fuck is that?" she blurted out without a single ounce of decorum.

Davis turned the ignition off and turned towards her and the children. "Let's go and meet the boss."

Chapter 34
1945

It was the beautiful, scenic journey from Offenburg to Zurich, and the swift but comfortable interchange in Switzerland for the train to Hungary that was giving Victor a false sense of security.

Their cabin on the Hungarian train was the most lavish he could buy. His cache at Zurich was bigger than his emergency stash at Offenburg. They would arrive at their favourite city in style, whether Gwen could appreciate it or not.

The first-class carriages teemed with elderly people, businessmen who were too old for national service, and inquisitive children. Victor felt like an imposter in the shabby clothes Hannalore had given them.

The other passengers dressed elegantly, in pretty dresses and pristine suits.

The dining carriage was crammed; people turned away when they saw him leading his wife by the arm and looking for somewhere to sit.

Gwen had deteriorated since the change of trains, something that had been happening more and more, especially when fatigue got the better of her.

She needed to rest.

Victor was about to turn and head back to their cabin when someone called out to them.

A middle-aged woman with steel-grey hair beckoned them from a table where she sat with a preteen boy and girl. "Please. There is room to sit with us, if you don't mind sharing with children?"

Victor thanked the lady and led Gwen to a seat.

"This is Kristof," the woman said, introducing the boy.

He was fair-haired, wore a three-piece grey suit, speckled with pastry flakes. They fell to the floor when he stood and offered Victor his hand. "How do you do, sir?"

"Pleased to make your acquaintance," Victor beamed; the boy had a firm grip. He nodded to the girl. "And who is this pretty young lady?"

"Gertrude," the girl said, cheeks flushing. "But most people call me Trudy."

"I'm Evelyn," the woman said, and offered her hand.

Victor made his own introductions and gave them a brief summary of Gwen's condition, about which Evelyn sympathised as her own mother had suffered similarly. They sat down and the woman explained to him how she was the children's aunt and private tutor.

Victor gave nothing away; he knew to keep the woman talking about her own life and to skirt any questions that came his way.

When the food arrived, Evelyn insisted that she help with Gwen as they had already eaten.

Victor picked up the cutlery and let out a small whelp. He dropped it back down immediately.

"What's wrong?" the woman asked, a soup spoon halfway to Gwen's lips.

He sucked in air through his teeth and carefully wrapped the cutlery in a cloth napkin. "My wife and I have a severe allergy to certain types of metal." He rubbed his fingers against his thighs. "We come out in terrible contact dermatitis."

Trudy looked disgusted and her brother peered at Victor's hand in expectation.

Victor smiled wanly and showed Kristof his blistering fingertips.

"Oh, Heavens," said Evelyn, and before Victor could add another word she called for one of the passing waiting staff.

Once the problem was sorted with cutlery sets from the lower-class carriages, Gwen let Evelyn feed her whilst she watched the scenery rush past the window.

Victor found he had the appetite of a ravenous beast and the children looked on in awe at the volume of food he devoured.

Dessert came. A young waitress wheeled a brass trolley, laden with different sundries, through the carriage. Victor smiled at her and clapped his hands, exaggerating his excitement for the children's amusement. Passengers shuffled patiently behind her in the dark confines between coaches, steadying themselves against the jolting of the train, waiting for an opportunity to slide past.

As the waitress wheeled the trolley further into the carriage, the people behind her moved into the light and all thoughts of ice cream or gateau zapped from Victor's mind.

It was the SS commander from Offenburg.

He gave a slow, cat-like grin and waved a leather-gloved hand over the waitress's shoulder.

FERAL

Chapter 35

Danny shrieked as an arc of boiling water splashed across his chest and Tony fell against the worktop and down to the floor.

Cyril lunged at him, his hands around his throat, and pushed him to the floor alongside his brother. Cyril landed on top of him, focusing his weight on one knee and pushing it into Danny's groin. This, added to the pain of the scalding water, made the edges of his vision darken and he almost blacked out.

Cyril forced his thumbs against Danny's windpipe, his spherical face bright red and his horrid little grey teeth clenched with the exertion.

He squeezed.

Danny's vision exploded with black dots; he clawed at Cyril, reaching for his face, but the man's arms were too long for him to reach.

Tony was up and wrapped an arm around the assailant's neck.

Cyril's strength was insane; for someone so awkward, his coordination and reactions were scarily quick, and he wore an expression of enjoyment, as though he were getting off on the struggle. This was the type of scenario where he could allow his true colours to show. He sprung up, Tony riding him in an aggressive piggyback, and slammed himself backwards against the nearest cupboard. Danny searched for a weapon: they may have been in a kitchen but it was a virtually empty kitchen with the bare minimum. He grabbed the first solid-looking object within reach, a toaster, slid his fingers into the bread slots, ripped the plug from the wall and smashed the thing into Cyril's face. His nose exploded and Danny felt several of his fingers snap inside the metal grill.

Cyril staggered forward; one hand went to his injured nose and the other tried to pry Tony's forearm from around his throat.

There was nothing for them to defend themselves with.

Danny felt his bones grating together as they reformed.

Cyril tried to reach Tony to get him off his back; he grabbed handfuls of his hair and yanked.

Danny ran at them, driving his shoulder into Cyril, but he thumped him in the ear and sent him reeling into the wall; his ear rang with the impact.

It was useless. Cyril was too big, his arms and legs seemed to be everywhere.

Danny turned back to scream, to attack, to do anything other than give in to the lanky freak.

A squeal penetrated the kitchen. Tony was still latched onto him like a baby monkey but now his mouth was pressed to the pale flesh of Cyril's neck.

Cyril batted at him with his fists, blood seeped from around Tony's lips, and he finally managed to get him off his back and threw him onto the floor.

Tony spat out a mouthful of gore.

Blood gushed from the wound in Cyril's throat; when he saw it he began mewling like a kid. Red splattered the cupboards as Cyril reverted to his nervous persona. He regarded them with so much fear in his eyes that a dark wet patch spread across the crotch of his beige slacks.

Tony staggered away from him, gagging on his blood, and moved out of the way as Cyril collapsed, pale-faced, to the tiles.

"What the hell do we do now?" Danny shouted, bug-eyed.

Despite Cyril's attempt to drug them and kill them, they couldn't stand by and watch him bleed out on the kitchen floor.

Tony took his t-shirt off, wadded it up, and pressed it against the wound in Cyril's neck. It wasn't as bad as it looked.

Cyril slumped against a cupboard, his skin waxen and glazed with sweat and blood. When he spoke it was barely audible. "What are you going to do with me?"

Danny jerked towards him. "You drugged us and attacked us, you fucking freak. We should let you bleed out and die right there on the floor."

Cyril grinned. "Do it."

"No," Tony snapped, "we are not like you." He pulled the cotton away from Cyril's throat; the bleeding was slowing.

He needed to get rid of the taste of the man. "Danny, hold this here whilst I find something better to restrain him with."

"Oh, it's been a while since we used restraints, Tony," Cyril said, leering at the half-naked skinny boy with blood on him.

"Shut the fuck up," Danny said, and took over from his brother.

Tony stared at their prisoner coldly. "If he tries anything, call out."

He left them and went into the cellar; Cyril followed him with his eyes and a sickening grin. When he had gone, he turned those bulbous orbs on Danny. "I bet you look even better without your top, too."

"Fuck off," Danny sneered, and pressed his fingertips hard into his wound.

"You could make some money, just like Tony does." His eyes closed at some pleasurable memory. "You'd be surprised by the things we've done."

"Shut up," Danny said through gritted teeth.

Cyril raised a shaking hand towards him.

Danny batted it away. "He only did that shit so he could get away from Boxford."

Cyril smiled weakly and shook his head. "Oh, no, you're wrong. He loves it. Loves the adoration, the attention, being wanted. He'll never stop, never give it up."

"Just shut the fuck up."

"He's so good at sucking cock," Cyril said lustfully. "Mmm. I bet you'd be good at it, too."

"I'm not listening."

"Ignore him, he's just trying to goad you into doing something stupid," Tony said, coming from the cellar wearing a clean top and carrying a pair of handcuffs. "Grab his hands."

Danny grimaced; Cyril's skin was cold and clammy.

"Ooh," Cyril sighed as Tony fastened the cuffs, "this is a dream come true."

Tony rolled his eyes.

"What are we going to do with him?" Danny asked, wiping his hands on his trousers.

"We just leave him. That bite mark isn't that bad. The cops will find him once we're away and call them about Tepes' stuff."

"Let me help you," Cyril said earnestly. "I know where there's more stuff. Money, drugs."

"We don't need your help," Tony said with contempt. "You've helped us enough already by supplying us with a getaway vehicle." Tony patted the pockets of Cyril's trousers until he felt his car keys. He plucked them out and placed them on the worktop.

Danny was impressed with Tony's thinking. A few months back, he would never have thought his brother capable of this kind of thing.

As they stood and stared down at the pathetic freak of a man, he wondered just how deep this was all going to get.

Would they ever be able to stop running?

What if he only created more problems; should he go at it alone, take the money and run?

Within twenty-four hours, he would be turning into a monster.

What the hell was going to happen if he couldn't contain it?

FERAL

Chapter 36
1945

Time slowed to an excruciating pace.

The waitress serving the desserts moved aside to allow the SS commander and a clutch of soldiers through. He locked eyes on Victor, making sure recognition passed both ways. To Victor's surprise, though, he continued through the carriage without uttering one word of acknowledgement.

His unease must have shown; Evelyn spoke softly once the men had gone. "I'm sure they are only here as a precaution."

Victor forced a smile. "Since my wife became ill, the sight of soldiers unnerves her. I am naturally apprehensive."

Victor cursed himself for having told Evelyn their real names, although it was likely the commander knew exactly who they were. He was probably under orders to follow them.

Victor wondered when they would finally be apprehended.

Would they be forced from the train at gunpoint at the next station or would their torture be prolonged for the entire trip to Budapest?

The waitress set down their desserts and Victor knew this was probably the last time he and Gwen would dine together.

Victor sat opposite Gwen in the small, comfortable cabin.

There was no more sign of the commander or the soldiers during their meal.

He managed to keep his anxiety under control in front of Evelyn and her children but in the privacy of their compartment, it came crashing down like a lead balloon.

It was futile.

He knew he wouldn't be able to fulfil his dying wish for Gwen: seeing Budapest one last time.

Gwen lay on the bottom of the bunk bed. He helped her get ready for sleep; she was quiet the whole time, as though she were in some kind of trance.

She fell asleep almost immediately.

He watched her, knowing they wouldn't see their favourite city again. "It's okay, I won't let them lay a hand on you."

Victor leant forward and kissed her on the cheek. "Sleep well, my sweet," he said, and slipped a pillow out from beneath her head.

He wasn't one hundred percent sure it would work, but it would hopefully spare her the pain of what was bound to follow.

Victor took the package from his pocket and unfolded the napkin holding the cutlery that had burned him earlier.

The silver and the sharpness of the steak knife would finish the job. With one last lingering glance at the woman he loved, he lowered the pillow over her face.

Chapter 37

The man should not be alive.

Charlotte couldn't diagnose what ailed him; aside from his emaciated appearance, she guessed he was in the final stages of something most definitely terminal.

His skin was shrunken and jaundiced, an oxygen mask covered his mouth and nose, intravenous drips grew from the wheelchair like strange fauna.

Sat in his behemoth of a chair, he was a science-fiction villain, wired to a robot like one of the Doctor's nemeses.

Davis and Fry stopped in front of him as if they were about to offer Charlotte as a sacrifice to a mechanical messiah.

The man in the wheelchair raised a withered hand that shook with some kind of palsy, and lightly brushed his fingertips against the screen by his chest. A voice, artificial and booming, came out of unseen speakers hidden amongst his contraption. "Take the children into the facility."

Davis signalled to some soldiers. "What about her?" he said, cocking a thumb at Charlotte.

She saw the man's red-rimmed eyes flit across her as if she was nothing, whilst he tapped at his screen.

"Lock her up in the barracks. We might need her as a bargaining chip."

"What the hell is going on here?" Charlotte asked the decrepit old man. Behind her, the cries of Kiran and Kayleigh came as the soldiers dragged them from the van.

FERAL

People in medical scrubs and pushing a pair of gurneys came out of the building and rushed towards them.

The old man's eyes blazed with cruel, cold excitement as the fighting twins were restrained, then once again they lit on her. "Lock her up."

Davis and Fry each took an arm and pulled her away from the man and the building. She saw him smile behind his mask.

*

They locked her up like a prisoner, in a room with just a bunk, a toilet and a sink.

No one had come back since the night before and she was starving.

As much as the governor teased her about it, the situation really was like something out of The X-Files.

They had taken the children and had tried to murder their mother. Charlotte thought about the recent attacks around Boxford, how they had been blamed on hoodlums and a bunch of pensioners. How all the ludicrous claims of werewolf attacks were quashed. No one in their right minds would have believed such a thing.

But what was the truth?

The twins were the grandchildren of one of the missing old folk, and even though the papers mentioned a mass funeral pyre in the park, nothing else had been mentioned about the bodies. To her knowledge, they hadn't been brought to her hospital, either.

Something important was being covered up and the more she dwelled on it, the less ludicrous the claims seemed to be.

Whatever was happening, there were people who were prepared to kill to keep it secret.

The way the men had shot the innocent bystanders with no hesitation made her wonder if she was just as expendable—

A jangle of keys brought her from her thoughts.

A soldier came in carrying a tray with a hot drink and a slice of toast. He put the tray down on the bed next to her without a word and made to leave.

"Oi," Charlotte snapped. The soldier looked at her half-heartedly. "How long am I going to be kept here?"

"As long as Butcher wants you here," he said, and turned to leave.

"Who the fuck is this guy?"

The solider paused in the open doorway and shrugged. "I have no idea. I'm just a dogsbody, but I know he's someone high up."

"What's going on here? Where are the kids that were brought in?"

"Again, I don't know." He started to pull the door closed. "I'm sure you'll be told all about it. Don't worry, I doubt they'll waste a doctor."

"That's such a reassurance, thanks," Charlotte's voice oozed sarcasm.

Voices echoed from somewhere outside the room.

The soldier stood to attention and spoke from the corner of his mouth. "Here comes the man himself."

Charlotte heard the soft purr of an electric motor.

The soldier stood aside as Sir Jonathan Butcher came through the door.

FERAL

Chapter 38

Juliet didn't have a plan; that was the problem, just to get to the place where her kids were and demand to be let in.

The barracks weren't far away but they may as well have been on the other side of the country, especially when relying on public transport.

She had to catch a train to a remote station she had never heard of. From then on, she would have to walk across several miles of winding country roads before she reached her destination, but she didn't care.

The rhythmic motion of the train made her fight hard against fatigue.

She hadn't slept properly for what felt like months.

Every time she blinked, her eyelids stayed closed a little bit longer, twice she dropped the bag containing the modified torch.

When she alighted at the small station, she checked the directions and began walking along roads which had no pavements.

It felt strange for someone so used to town life to be surrounded by so much greenery.

The last time she had seen so much countryside was when she and her dad had taken the twins to Barmouth the previous summer.

Just thinking about her dad brought tears to her eyes.

Back then, he couldn't even walk a mile without complaining about his knees and needing to sit down, but they managed. Kiran and Kayleigh were just as bad, and he was perpetually happy around them.

He would hold their hands and make them laugh with tales of his childhood in Jamaica, their mother growing up, how things were so different back then, even more so when he and their gran moved to Boxford. The twins weren't born when she was alive, but they had heard one or two things about Granny Dolores from Jamal and Jeanelle.

They fired questions at him about this legendary figure they'd never got to meet and he told them how she was gazing down from the stars, watching them grow.

In turn, they made him cackle by waving and blowing kisses up at the clouds.

Juliet remembered the conversation they'd had on Barmouth beach.

The weather was blowing a gale, but it didn't stop them from going on the sand.

They sat with their feet turning blue whilst Kiran and Kayleigh raced around looking for shells, crabs, and other delights the channel had left behind for them to discover.

"This will be the last time I see the coast," he had said, resting his hands on his knees and sighing.

"Pfft." She recognised what would be the beginning of one of his morbid rants about age and death, a regular thing since her mother had passed away. "Why? Are our trips not good enough for you? Would you rather be down the pub with Norman, moaning and getting maudlin about the good old days that weren't, when you think about it, all that good?"

"Woman—"

"Don't you *woman* me, Dad. You gave me a name, use it."

He sighed. "I'm old. I'm not long for this world. I can feel it in me bones."

"Oh, please," she scoffed. "You've been saying this for the last decade."

"I mean it," he insisted. "The Reaper is sharpening his scythe, I can almost hear it."

"Give me a break. I'm sure the secret to longevity is bloody well moaning and saying you're going to die soon."

He shook his head slowly.

"Oh for goodness' sake, why are you getting like this? We're on holiday! Aren't you enjoying yourself?"

He watched the twins chasing one another across the shoreline. "There are so many things I wish I could have done."

She rolled her eyes. "Like what? Run a marathon? Get married again? What?"

"My running days are over, dead and gone."

"Dad, I don't think they were ever alive."

His face lit and his laughter was louder than the wind. Two spots far off over the wet sand grew back into children as they hurtled towards them with their buckets swinging.

"You know the only woman for me was your mother," he said, nudging her with his shoulder and winking. "Although, I suppose Beyoncé would make an okay second wife."

"Dad! She's less than half your age!"

"Okay then, she can double up with that hot little number from that programme Jamal was watching last time he came, the one with that man who has an arsehole for a mouth." He roared with the memory of the character in his grandson's programme.

She shook her head with fake disbelief, happy he was being more like himself. "Two wives? That really would be the end of you. They'd bloody kill you."

"What a way to go."

"You're a dirty old man," she said, slapping his thigh.

As Kiran and Kayleigh got closer, they saw how covered they were with muddy sand.

Kiran carried a massive clump of seaweed that looked like a witch's wig.

"I just wish I could see my home one more time," he said, going back to moping. "To sit like this on Montego Bay sharing a rum with the Caribbean Sea."

"It *would* be nice to see where you and Mum grew up," she added, feeling herself grow maudlin.

Her mum had always intended to return to Jamaica, one big lavish holiday, to dig up forgotten relatives and show off the family she had created in England.

But it never happened.

"I doubt I'd recognise the place now."

"Let's go."

He laughed some more. "Sure thing, Ju."

"No, Dad, I mean it. Jamal and Jeanelle are grown-ups, they can pay for themselves. Let's take the kids, show them their heritage."

His smile vanished; there was a brief glimpse of hope behind his eyes before it vanished. "Nah, man, I'm old, too old for that. The flight alone would kill me, and we can't afford it."

"Wouldn't you rather die over the sunny Caribbean than sat next to Norman in the pub after six too many?"

"You think we could? We could really do it?" His excitement, the way his face was animated behind his beard, made him look just like Kiran.

"Old man, we can do anything we set our hearts and minds to. And if you cark it whilst we're over there, at least Death will get some sun on his bones."

Kiran skidded to a halt at their feet and the conversation turned to seashells and seaweed. She had meant every word of it, whether he believed her or not, and saved every penny from then on.

Now what would happen?

She eyed the checkpoint at the barracks gate, saw the soldiers and their guns and all thoughts of bravado washed away as quickly as the memory of her dad at Barmouth.

She took the Maglite from her bag and put it in a nearby bin.

Reckless behaviour would get her killed, not get her children back.

FERAL

Chapter 39

It was hard investigating Cyril's background but Bartholomew researched anyone he let into his circle.

The jibe about Samuel Ellington was purely that, a joke.

All he managed to find out about Cyril's younger years was that he had hung around boys half his age, and that one lad who was regularly seen with Cyril was Samuel, who had gone missing.

Bluebell Woods used to be a hot-spot for young couples at night. He put two and two together and it wasn't hard to know there was something off about the man.

Bartholomew knew, as though there was a telepathic connection enabling him to sense other killers. In a way they were alike, despite their different proclivities.

He sensed Cyril had killed more than once, but suspected he hadn't indulged for a long time. He had seen it build up inside him every time Tony was mentioned; he held it back like a feral animal. After everything was over with the Scarborough boys, maybe it would be good to find out every last detail of the man's chequered past.

Bartholomew considered his own history and the volume of incriminating evidence in his house and work yard.

Bodies in freezers: his keepsakes.

It was highly likely Cyril would have questions of his own.

FERAL

Most of the night, he lay awake imagining Cyril doing his thing, waiting for the phone call to say the job was done, that the brothers were dead.

Breakfast came and went.

If something had gone wrong, the police would have been able to connect everything to him by now. He gave up waiting and rang Cyril's number and the call went straight through to voicemail.

With each passing hour, Bartholomew became more and more frustrated. He understood how certain individuals, such as he and Cyril, could get carried away with their little games and rituals, but when it got to the twenty-four-hour mark, he decided to take matters into his own hands.

Bartholomew got out of bed.

Apart from feeling physically drained, and his one leg being weaker than before, he felt fine. He drew the curtains around the bed and began to get dressed.

It was time for the vampire to rise from the grave.

*

Danny felt euphoric, as though he could smash through walls or scale tall buildings. He knew it was the thing inside him making sure he was in prime condition for its debut appearance.

Tony had been back to Tepes' stash and had bought weed with some of the cash. "I have no idea if this will help," he said, holding up a small package.

Danny nodded towards Cyril, where he lay curled on his side appearing to sleep. "Watch what you say. I don't think our guest is really asleep."

Cyril's bleeding had stopped and even though they had no intention of letting him go, Tony made him drink sugary tea and fed him like a baby.

Cyril sickened Danny; he could tell the man got off on Tony mothering him, and the longer they kept him prisoner, the cockier he got.

Cyril knew they wouldn't hurt him; they hadn't the guts. They were wanted for some gang-related stuff so even if they did hand him in, they wouldn't stick around. They would take whatever it was Tepes had stashed away and run, contacting the police anonymously when they were far away.

Without the brothers, his own punishment wouldn't be so severe, but everything would come out about Tepes and his little operation with the brothels, and Tepes had made it more than clear that if he were to go down, so would Cyril.

He opened his eyes. "Can you help me sit up, please?"

Tony slipped the weed in his pocket and gestured for Danny to assist.

"So, are you two just going to get stoned and keep me prisoner?"

"I need to check his wound," Tony said, ignoring him and putting a hand to the gauze on his neck. After they restrained him, Tony patched him up properly.

"You realise Tepes is going to kill you if you take his stuff, don't you?" he said, revelling in their fear. "Yeah, he knows you've been snooping. His place is alarmed, he knows your every move."

Tony withdrew from him. "He's not going anywhere, the state he's in."

"He has connections." Cyril smiled. "Loads of connections."

Tony laughed. "You don't know anything. You're just a sad old man."

"Oh, I know exactly what he's capable of," Cyril sneered. "I've known him for years."

"Do you know he's a serial killer?" Danny blurted.

"Danny!"

Cyril saw the horror on Tony's face, and knew he thought what Danny said was true. He was stunned by the revelation but a lot of things began to make sense. He began to laugh, a wheezing, high-pitched thing.

The two of them were as bad as each other, two peas in a pod.

It was no surprise that his own interests had never seemed to bother Tepes at all.

There was nothing else to be said; he knew how they would play this out. He just had to find a way to escape before they contacted the police.

He pursed his virtually non-existent lips together and blew Tony a kiss.

"Fuck you." Tony spat in Cyril's face, the saliva landing on his sunken cheek.

Cyril stuck his grey tongue out to gather it up. "Any other bodily fluids you want to throw at me?"

"Come on." Tony grabbed Danny by the arm and marched him toward the cellar.

Chapter 40
1945

The pillow was over Gwen's face for a full minute before she made any attempt at fighting, and even then, it was feeble.

Tears blurred Victor's vision and rained on the cotton pillowcase.

He pushed down harder.

Gwen batted at his face, the first time in their marriage that one had struck the other.

A fingernail flensed the skin of his cheek and he lost hold for a second.

It was enough.

A surge of power rippled through her like an electric shock. Her pelvis bucked and she threw him off.

He crashed against a small hand basin, his head striking the porcelain, and slid to the floor.

Gwen came at him like a mad woman.

Bright intelligence shone from her suddenly-yellow eyes. Her clothes began to split and her skin darkened with sprouting grey fur.

"Oh God, what have I done?" Victor groaned. Blood ran down his head.

Her transformation was rapid.

Within a matter of seconds, a hulking great monster filled the small cabin. Its triangular head yawned, revealing long yellow teeth.

Even as Victor beheld the sight of his wife in wolf form, she seemed to grow bigger.

She growled and rose from the bed, bipedal.

"Gwen, no!" Victor shouted, still on the floor. She leapt the few feet between them and towered over him. She raised a paw bigger than his head, ready to strike.

Victor felt his own beast rear up inside him; bones and muscles manipulated themselves to make him a more worthy opponent.

His monster rushed to the surface.

An eruption of grey fur burst through his subcutaneous layers and he roared with the pain of it all.

Gwen slashed a paw across his chest; the claws separated material and flesh with ease.

The agony of her attack slowed his change and sapped his fight.

He flung himself away from her, and in an explosion of cloth, blood, and bone, his wolf emerged ready to defend.

Victor sprang onto the bed to avoid another one of Gwen's swipes.

Both of their reflexes were lightning-fast.

Their talons carved great furrows in the cabin walls as they battled; a collision of fur, tooth, and claw.

Voices outside the cabin distracted them as muzzles sought throats to tear. There was frantic banging and then something wedged in the door to break the lock. The door slid across, and a couple of soldiers recoiled from the sight in front of them.

The SS commander peered over the heads of half a dozen men and shouted for them to fire.

The soldiers' reactions were too slow, no match for those of the Lycan. Gwen threw herself through the doorway, barrelling into them before they had a chance to raise their guns. Within seconds, the narrow corridor was awash with blood.

Seeing better, easier prey, Gwen loped off after the retreating soldiers through the carriages.

Victor thought about the innocent people on board: Evelyn, Kristof, and Trudy, and gave chase.

Screaming and gunfire rang through the train as a surge of passengers fled the oncoming slaughter.

Gwen ripped apart everyone in immediate reach; the air was a visceral red mist of blood and skin. She raked their backs as they ran through the narrow thoroughfare.

Victor saw her clamp her jaws down on a fleeing man's head, biting off the back of it from crown to neck. His brain was visible for a second before he fell forward like a domino and brought down a woman ahead of him.

Her claws dug furrows in the seats. She moved after them at a slowed pace due to the narrow aisle.

The remaining soldiers seized the opportunity to turn and shoot, not caring if passengers got in the line of fire. She reared up on her hind legs and roared, bullets peppering her chest and torso. Victor sprang at her and wrapped his arms around her chest in a bear hug. Bullets lanced into his forearms and shoulders. Despite the pain, the wounds healed as quickly as they were made.

Gwen shook him off her back with such force he obliterated one of the dining room tables and smashed through a window. Cold, rushing air. A heavy weight landed on him.

Gwen's triangular head burst through the remaining glass, her fur matted and red, and she lowered her blood-foamed fangs towards his throat. He pushed back at her, his moves more defence than attack, and tried to get back into the carriage.

The struggle caused him to slip further, closer to the rails. If she got him completely off the locomotive, all hope would be lost; he'd never catch up.

Ahead, he saw a thick metal post by the rail side; he wrapped one arm around Gwen and latched onto it as it passed. They were ripped from the train, and for a split second it sped on without them, but Gwen, not wanting to let such a plentiful food supply get away, grabbed hold of one of the passing carriage door handles, something that would surely amputate a normal person's arm, and flipped onto the train roof.

Victor fell to the siding, where stone, iron, and wood broke his bones and tried to destroy him. He rolled through dense foliage until he came to a standstill at the bottom of a steep embankment. Ignoring his battered body, he bounded up the slope on all fours and landed on the line in time to see the train vanish into the distance.

Chapter 41

"I can feel it coming," Danny said with ominous excitement.

The cellar was painted black, with numerous whips, chains and harnesses decorating the walls.

A bare mattress on a metal frame had enough restraints to immobilise a person.

"What the hell?" Danny said when he saw a display cabinet full of lethal-looking sex toys.

Tony couldn't contain his amusement. "It's a bit grim, isn't it?" He pointed to what looked exactly like an electric chair: there was even a head clamp. "This won't be the most comfortable thing but the restraints are probably the strongest in the room."

"This is fucking sick." Danny was disgusted, he didn't want to know about half the things that went on down here.

"I know, but there isn't any other option."

Danny sat down on the reinforced chair.

"Now, I know you said you can feel it coming, but I take it you don't mean now? I mean, nothing is happening that I can see."

"It's like when you feel you're coming down with something like the 'flu, but the opposite. I can feel it rising inside of me as if I'm going to explode."

Tony checked his watch. "Well, as neither of us know anything about this, and the calendar says it's the full moon today, I think we ought to get started." He plucked a neon pink bong from a nearby shelf and waggled it about.

"What if these straps don't hold?" Danny said, inspecting one of the metal wrist clamps on the chair arms.

"The cellar door will be bolted and that door is solid as fuck." Doubt began to register on Tony's face. "Other than that, hopefully you'll be too fucked to do anything." He filled the bong and set about lighting it.

Danny slumped in the chair and flopped his wrists against the cuffs. "Let's just get this over with."

Tony fastened the restraints and held the bong towards Danny so he could take a hit. "I'm not undoing these until the morning, you know that, right?"

"What if I need a piss?" Danny blurted through blue vapour.

"I expect things will get a little messy but it's okay, this whole place is one big wet room." He pointed to a drain in the centre of the floor.

Danny grimaced and pressed his mouth against the bong; he could feel the effects of the drug already.

*

"I think it's happening," Danny whined. He looked so young, like he did when they were kids. Tony remembered when they used to play together, back when Danny looked up to him, before things got complicated.

They were playing on the grounds at the Green Man Estate. The council had organised some sort of shindig to celebrate so many years of the estate. Everybody was given a token for a hot dog that one of the caretakers was barbecuing. There was a bouncy castle and live music.

Everyone was on their best behaviour but the estate wasn't that bad then; most of the GMC were Danny's age or hadn't been taken under Neep's wing yet. A small under-12s play area had been put in that summer and it was the main doss area for most of the kids. They went down there whenever their dads got drunk or the four walls of their flats closed in too much.

Danny was showing off to a couple of other kids whilst he sat nearby. The grounds were alive with noise and merriment, adult banter, kids running riot. He watched the revellers, the cheesy man and woman singing on a makeshift stage, and didn't see Danny standing on top of the climbing frame like Spider-Man. Just as he was about to call out, Danny lost his balance and fell twelve feet to the ground. He ran into the park, past the shocked children, expecting to see his brother's brains spread over the concrete, but Danny stood there as if it was nothing, shrugging and faking laughter. He strutted away from them coolly, pretending he was fine, but when Danny saw Tony and the bruise began blossoming on one side of his face, Tony saw the real fight in his eyes, the struggle of holding back tears.

Sweat poured off Danny. Tony felt an intense fever-heat coming off him. "Jesus, you're burning up."

"It feels like there are ants beneath my skin," Danny grimaced.

"We should have stripped you off." Tony had seen these things change.

"Fuck off," Danny spat, "I ain't sitting on this thing in the buff. Christ knows what's on it."

"As seedy as you might think this place is, we do keep it clean, you know?"

Danny started to say something but pain suddenly tore across his abdomen and made him cry out.

Tony stepped back; he wanted to comfort him but knew what was going to happen.

FERAL

Danny's heart was beating so fast it was one continuous pulsation. Fire raged beneath his skin; his nerve endings screamed. "It's coming," he managed, before something cracked in his jaw and his whole head exploded.

"Just fight it, Danny," Tony said feebly, but didn't know how the hell anyone could fight such a thing.

Danny's whole body went rigid in the chair, his skin beaded with blood-tinged sweat, his lips peeled back and thick red foam bubbling out between his splintering teeth. "It's tearing me apart," he screamed, and a torrent of thick, claret gruel gushed from his mouth. His arms ballooned beneath his shirt; the skin ripped and saturated the material in an instant. His head reared back, and his mouth opened in a scream that literally tore his face in two. His eyes burst in their sockets and oozed away to make space for twin feral yellow orbs. His wolf ripped him apart.

*

Bartholomew made it as far as the corridor outside the ward before his leg felt like it would give way. He braced himself against the wall and hobbled towards the exit. He rounded a corner and headed towards Accident and Emergency.

When people noticed his difficulties, they assumed he was another emergency case.

A nurse pulled a sympathetic face, rushed into the reception area, and returned with a crutch. He took it and carried on through the milling crowd. Outside, a taxi spilled more injured at the entrance. As they got out, he got in.

"I've got another job," the young driver said, incredulous. "I can't just pick people up. You have to book."

"I'll pay you double," Bartholomew snapped, and the driver shrugged and drove away.

*

Cyril backed into the cupboards and drawers and tried yanking them open with his cuffed hands. *There has to be something I can use to pick these bloody things.* He moaned with frustration, finding nothing but a few packets of instant noodles. Nothing of use at all. He leant against the counter, grabbed his car keys and banged his head against the cheap wood. Then he saw it: the key sticking out of the secured back door. Tony hadn't removed it after his surprise visit the night before. He stepped across and blindly fumbled with the bolts and the lock. The night air hit him and promised answers to his predicament.

He knew there would be something in his car he could use. He twisted his hips around, for once thankful for his gangly physique, and pulled his car keys from his trouser pocket.

The back garden was an overgrown junkyard; twice he stumbled and almost overbalanced. It was so dark; most of the streetlights down this end of the road had been vandalised years before. His nerves got the better of him as he pushed himself onwards around the house to where he'd left the car. It would be just his luck to turn the corner and see someone had nicked it. His usual shakes and tremors began and he stood still to try to compose himself; this wasn't the time for clumsiness. Cyril closed his eyes and thought about what he was going to do to the boys once he'd freed himself. If the cellar was as well-equipped as it had been during one of his more *specialised* visits, he would have the brothers trussed up like Christmas turkeys by the end of the night. The imagery of that calmed him. He turned the corner and laughed at the sight of the yellow peril right where he had left it. *Ha, not even joyriders would want to steal that embarrassing thing.*

He hurried over to it, keys in hand, moved around to the boot where his toolkit was kept, and a tall shadow appeared out of nowhere.

"'Ello, 'ello, 'ello, and where do you think you're going in such a hurry? Ha-ha."

Chapter 42

Butcher waited in the doorway to Charlotte 's room, where the four agents stood sentinel. "Doctor Smith," he said via his artificial aid, and nodded for Davis to continue.

Davis came into the room and smiled. "Hey, we've got a surprise roommate for you. They turned up about an hour ago." He stepped aside and two soldiers thrust Juliet towards Charlotte; a thick strip of duct tape was across her lips and she had her wrists zip-tied together.

Butcher fussed with his touchscreen. "You'll both join us later for the show."

"What the hell is he on about?" Charlotte asked.

Davis laughed but said nothing.

"Tell them," Butcher said, fixing his eyes on the two women.

Davis gestured for Charlotte and Juliet to sit.

"As you may have guessed, the rumours about werewolves running amok are one hundred percent true."

"Like hell," Charlotte scoffed.

Davis chuckled. "Oh, come on, Doctor, you've seen the results from tests you made on the children. Their remarkable healing abilities."

Juliet whined from behind the tape.

Charlotte leant across and peeled it off.

She wet her lips and spoke. "My babies are not monsters."

Butcher gave a toothless grin.

"Oh, we'll see about that later," Davis said.

FERAL

"You can't expect me to believe this," Charlotte said coldly, but one look at Juliet told her she, at least, was willing to, now.

"Well, like I said, whether you believe it or not is irrelevant. You will have all the evidence you need tonight."

"What's happening later?"

"The full moon."

Charlotte shook her head. "This is ridiculous."

"I know," Davis grinned. "They still haven't quite worked out the whole moon thing yet."

"What are you going to do to my children?" Juliet asked.

"We're going to stop your children from turning into mindless monsters."

Juliet laughed at the incredulity of his statement. "So why try and have me killed if you planned on helping them?"

Charlotte had a creeping suspicion.

"Oh," Davis said, sharing a look with Butcher. "We are obviously going to help them, that's true. We're going to help them control the thing inside them." Again, he turned to his boss to seek his approval.

The cadaverous man gave the slightest of nods.

Davis continued, "We're going to teach them how to control their beasts so they can work for us. There's a war coming."

*

Charlotte listened in a state of shock as Juliet explained everything that had happened since her dad and his friends had started acting weird. How he had suddenly gone from a moaning old man to one who had sudden unexplained outbursts of energy, which he laughably put down to clean living.

Juliet ended things with, "It's just hard to believe that what we thought were fictional monsters are real."

"I refuse to believe it until I see it," Charlotte said, pacing the room. "Just because they use the term 'werewolf' doesn't mean they're what we're thinking of. It can't be. I mean, clinical lycanthropy, maybe."

"You're a woman of science," Juliet said, "surely you can't deny what you found out yourself. Kiran's appendix."

"I'm more inclined to believe they never took the thing out in the first place. There's such a thing as bad surgeons."

"Don't you think all these stories, these myths and legends, have some basis in truth?"

"Yeah, of course. But the closest things are porphyria, hypertrichosis, or, like I said, clinical lycanthropy. There has been extensive research into regenerative medicine for decades and, with the right type of stimulus, there are certain parts of the body that can regenerate, but nothing on this scale."

"My children were found covered in blood. *Their own blood*. You said so yourself. And there was little scarring. I don't want this to be true, really I don't. Because if it is, then it means my dad was a monster too and that he tried to kill my children. You say there are things close to this—"

"Yeah, but nothing so blatant anyone would think they're *actual* monsters. Well, not in this day and age."

"So, what if this is something new, rare, or something old that's been reintroduced?"

Charlotte shrugged. "Whatever it is, it's important enough for them to want to hush it up. To murder people. We need to get out of here, go to the press, or something."

Juliet rested her hand on Charlotte 's arm. "I agree, but first we need to get my babies."

"How the hell do we do that? I don't know if you've noticed, but I'm built like a stick insect and have spent far too many years in medical books rather than martial arts texts."

"Doctor Smith —"

"Charlotte."

"Charlotte. I'm an extremely pissed-off mother. Werewolves or not, I am going to get my babies out of this place one way or another. You said these men carry guns. We don't have to be karate experts or ninjas. We just have to get one of their guns off them. All I want to know is whether you'll help me or not."

Charlotte stared at her, impressed by her steely determination, and nodded.

Chapter 43

Danny's wolf was wiry and lean. It looked malnourished, anorexic compared to the other beasts Tony had seen, with their bulging muscles and broad chests. It struggled at the bonds, the leather creaking with the strain; if he had been any bigger, they probably would have held. It roared and gnashed its teeth at him, tendons stretched in its sparsely furred neck.

"Danny, if you can hear me, you have to find a way to fight this. Show it that you are in charge."

The beast glowered at him with hungry, malevolent yellow eyes.

"Think of Dad. Think of Mum. You can do it. Make it stop." Tony didn't know if he was getting through, or whether it was even possible for Danny to take control over this, but he knew that others controlled theirs so there must be a way. If it wasn't a battle of wills, what was it? The wolf ripped its head back and bellowed in what sounded like pain, a canine whine.

"That's it, Danny."

The wolf's growling whine turned into a strangulated whimper and it began to thrash about more vigorously, one last attempt to free itself. It began to change but fought all the way. The elongated muzzle kept crumpling in on itself, splitting and ejecting razor-sharp fangs, the fur retreating back into the scalp before it regrew, painfully. Tony watched with fascination as its discarded bits on the floor shrivelled away to nothing. The head collapsed in on itself, as though it had been hit with a sledgehammer; the noise it made was half-animal, half-human, mangled reforming brain oozing through dislocated bones like passata. Tony heard something that sounded vaguely like his brother and watched as the bloody mess started to meld into a human skull, the muscles and skin forming in milliseconds. The squelching and crunching of flesh knitting together was sickening. Gradually, the wolf form retreated and Danny flopped forward in the chair, naked and spent.

Tony approached him cautiously. He didn't know whether he should release him or not. There was no telling how long this transformation stage would last for. Gingerly, he put his hand to Danny's chest, ready to pull it away if there was any hint of the thing returning. The fever-heat had fled from him but he could feel his heart hammering. Goosebumps prickled the skin on his arms. Tony searched the cellar for something to throw over him, to at least keep him warm, but there was nothing. He didn't want to leave him until he was conscious. He was breathing and not currently a monster, that was the main thing. If they had to do this every full moon, then they would. As soon as Danny was over this, they would take Tepes' stuff and run. Once they were somewhere safe, he would tell the police what he had found at Tepes' house and the terrible things Cyril had done.

Danny let out a loud snore, and Tony sniggered with nervous laughter. If this was the end of the transformation, it wasn't half as bad as he thought it was going to be and Danny's wolf wasn't that much bigger than he was in human form. It was a little anticlimactic, though, especially considering how terrifying the others had been, although he didn't fancy his chances with the thing if it was unrestrained. All that pain and bloodshed to turn into something so weasly and pathetic. He remembered the red-furred wolf that had gone head-first into a car when they had fled the arboretum; it had been a quadruped, and not much bigger than a large dog, but it was as powerful as a tank so he knew these things shouldn't be underestimated and were obviously capable of different forms.

Tony turned from his sleeping brother and climbed up the cellar steps. There was no way he was going to free Danny until the morning but that didn't mean he had to sit there shivering all night. There would be stuff in the bedrooms to make him more comfortable. Just as he reached for the door handle, the door swung inwards, the side smacking him hard in the face and sending him back down the stairs. He grabbed the stair rail as he fell and felt his shoulder tear as he prevented himself from falling.

"Hello, boys," Tepes said, filling the doorway. Cyril leered over him, Jack Skellington made flesh. Tony righted himself and ran to the bottom of the steps. The two men came down and Tepes stopped when he saw Danny strapped in the bondage chair. He looked at Tony with a mixture of surprise and admiration, before turning to Cyril to gauge his reaction. However, the shock was short-lived, his familiar, yet slightly askew grin appeared, and so did his trademark laugh. "What have you pair been up to?"

FERAL

Chapter 44
1945

After running as fast as he could in wolf form for an hour, he found the train, dark and silent.

He padded alongside the string of carriages. There were windowpanes washed red and speckled with bullet holes.

The smell of blood was overpowering, so enticing that part of him that wanted to join in with Gwen's festivities, but he resisted it as he sought the window from which he had fallen and leapt onto the train.

The carriage had been obliterated, an explosion of destroyed furniture. Sodden fragments of skin and body parts were strewn all over the place, some of it still recognisable as the person it had once belonged to. Several bodies lay on their backs riddled with bullet holes. Victor stopped and saw young Trudy lying on her back on top of a headless corpse, a look of surprise on her beautiful face and a single bullet hole above her right eye. Ragged remains in front of her bore the tattered leftovers of her brother's suit. He found their aunt, at least what he thought was Evelyn, sprawled out across a dining table, her face a hollow cave and her torso a ruby ruin. There were some passengers who huddled in a group, crammed into one of the larger luggage compartments, they seemed to bear only minor scratches, but all had been assassinated professionally. The SS commander knew what he was dealing with. Victor slid back into human form. It felt alien after being a quadruped for hours. This condition was so remarkable, and yet so deadly. He wondered what its limits of transformation were. He waded naked through the massacre: another carriage, another bloodbath. There was so much visceral destruction it was impossible to tell who the remains belonged to, although conveniently he could make out a patch of black material and a bloodied swastika. That was one death he wouldn't mourn; the SS commander had had it coming to him. Something moved from behind a pile of shredded death. Covered head-to-toe in blood and purple chunks of gore, Gwen studied the stuff on her hands with a clarity Victor had not seen in months— if not years. She saw him, and for a brief second he saw his wife in her eyes, not the shuffling time-stuck living cadaver she had become. He collapsed and directed all his anguish and sorrow to her blood-slickened feet.

Chapter 45

Charlotte heard people approaching and hoped Butcher was with them; he was obviously the one in charge. They readied themselves.

Juliet held her breath as the door opened.

Two soldiers came in and without any hesitation she threw herself on to them.

One caught her almost immediately, his reactions fast, the other recoiled but instantly went to help his comrade.

Juliet was a woman possessed. She screamed, shrieked, and clawed at him. Then Charlotte stepped forward and kicked one of them squarely in the testicles. He doubled over as the other drove his fist into Juliet's solar plexus. She crumpled to the floor and he pounced on her, forcing her arms behind her back.

"Let her go," Charlotte said, holding the other soldier's automatic rifle, which she took off him as he clutched at his balls. "I don't know much about guns, but I do know that this is the trigger and this is the end I point away from myself." The injured soldier lunged for her but she jumped back and smiled at him. "And this," she said as she flicked a switch on the weapon, "is the safety."

"They're not even loaded," said the soldier pinning Juliet to the floor.

"Shall we put that to the test?" Charlotte forced a wry smirk on her face; it would hopefully go well with this new tough-girl persona. "My aim might not be that great but I do know of multiple places I can shoot you that will hurt like fuck but not actually kill you. Trust me, I'm a doctor." She aimed the gun at the soldier who had not long let go of his testicles. "Who wants to be the guinea pig?"

Both soldiers shook their heads and raised their hands. More flooded into the hall behind them; once they saw Charlotte with the gun, they stopped and some even had the audacity to laugh.

"Don't you fucking dare laugh at me," she screamed at their condescending faces. "I've been kidnapped, groped, and this woman's life has been threatened. Some big, top-secret bollocks is going down here. I'm willing to bet if I shot one or two of you not even your families would find out about it." Further footfall brought Davis and Spencer, who instantly reached into their jackets for the guns concealed there.

"Don't you dare!" Charlotte seethed.

Juliet got to her feet, took the other soldier's handgun, and held it against his head. "Take me to my children."

*

They followed the soldiers through the facility, Juliet pressing the pistol into her hostage's back, Charlotte doing the same with her soldier. They came to a large open area that overflowed with soldiers and medical personnel. Butcher sat amongst them. He showed no emotion when he saw Juliet and Charlotte. Three hospital beds were being moved somewhere by a line of people in scrubs, accompanied by armed guards. On the first bed was a man with cropped grey hair; behind him, Kiran and Kayleigh. They were all strapped down and unconscious.

"Ah, just in time." Butcher's voice echoed around the room from unseen speakers. Charlotte pointed her gun at his head. She nodded at Juliet. "Get your kids."

Juliet shoved the soldier away and ran to her children. She slapped their faces but neither roused. "What have you done to them?"

"It's time for their transformation," Davis said.

"Put them in your van or I'll shoot your boss right here," Charlotte shouted, stepping closer to him. The decrepit old man gave a hissing wheeze that she thought was laughter. "Do it," he said. It was the first time she had heard his actual voice and it was barely perceptible.

"You're making a huge mistake," Davis warned.

The medical personnel quickly wheeled the children towards the exit. Davis shook his head at Butcher's evident amusement and left the building to find transport.

The medical staff unbuckled the children's restraints with shaking hands, constantly under the gaze of the soldier and their automatic rifles as they were loaded into the back of Davis's transporter. Juliet jumped in the back with them and pushed her gun against his head.

Charlotte followed Butcher and watched as he tapped at his keyboard. Dozens of suggested words floated on the touch-screen before the artificial voice said them aloud, volume up to maximum. "Juliet, don't you want to know what happened to your father?"

Juliet leant back out of the van. Charlotte watched as Butcher opened up a box on his tablet and a clinical room appeared on the screen. On it were three figures wearing hospital gowns. They were all secured with heavy-duty restraints. Three men: two Caucasians and one person of colour like Juliet. Charlotte looked to her, deflated. "I think you need to see this."

Juliet swiped the tears away. "No, they brought this on themselves. Let's go."

Charlotte ran from Butcher, expecting a bullet to lance into her at any second. She slipped into the passenger seat and trained her gun on Davis. "Drive."

Davis drove away from Butcher and the facility towards the high wire gates. "We're all going to die."

Charlotte ignored him and focused on Juliet. "Are they okay? Still breathing?"

Juliet gasped. "I think they're waking up."

Davis wouldn't take his eyes off the mirror at whatever was going on in the back seat.

"Just concentrate on getting us out of here," Charlotte said, prodding him in the ribs with the gun.

"Fuck this," Davis said, "shoot me if you have to." He yanked the steering wheel hard to one side and Charlotte smashed her temple against the door frame. Everything swirled in an explosion of stars and the van stopped. Davis was gone in a heartbeat, across the tarmac back to Butcher.

"Charlotte," Juliet screamed, and leant into the front to check on the dazed doctor.

Charlotte touched a hand to her head; she had hit the door hard but there was no blood. She noticed the empty driving seat and Davis' distant running figure. They would come after them. "We need to go," she said, and slid over to take the wheel. She was right, she could hear the rumble of their vehicles approaching.

"Charlotte," Juliet said, faltering, "something's happening to my babies."

Charlotte spun around. The twins were convulsing. Blood-tinged foam coated their lips as their little bodies jolted on the back seat as though they were being electrocuted. Juliet spread her arms across their chests to try and still their thrashing.

"Shit," Charlotte swore. They had to get away, that was paramount. She switched the interior light on so she could examine them better and briefly check their airways. The rest would have to wait. Kiran's eyes snapped open and they weren't human; they were like a dog's, feral. The children's skin bubbled; it was as if they were slowly being roasted from within. Juliet stared at them with heartbroken finality and hugged them both towards her chest. Kayleigh's arms went rigid and her little hands widened, split and splayed as thick black talons burst from her fingertips. Juliet gasped at their transformation, the sounds of her children's bodies breaking and reforming in front of her eyes.

Charlotte was glued to their metamorphosis. Blood sprayed her face as Kiran and Kayleigh fully succumbed to their tiny wolf forms.

"Go!" Juliet shrieked.

Charlotte leapt from the van as the sounds of animalistic fury shook the suspension. She heard Juliet shriek, saw her lose her grip on the bucking monsters and vanish amidst a whirlwind of fur. Scores of soldiers came across the tarmac on foot and in jeeps with mounted machine guns. Some of the ones who came on foot carried flamethrowers.

Charlotte ran away from the rocking van and put her hands in the air.

FERAL

Chapter 46

Tony ran to Danny and started to undo his restraints. Tepes let Cyril past and he thundered down the stairs and wrapped one of his long arms around him. Tony twisted and squirmed in Cyril's headlock but then saw the carving knife he held and the ecstatic grin on his face. "Cyril, please."

"It's over, Tony," he said, touching the knife to his cheek.

Tony felt him push his crotch against his lower back, felt how excited he was. Tony leant back, pressing himself into him. "Please, I'll do anything."

"Oh," Tepes said, finally getting down the steps, "you'll be doing anything we want anyway by the time we're finished with you." Tepes hobbled over to Danny and pressed his fingers against the pulse in his neck. "What's going on here? Incest? You are brothers, aren't you?" He touched the rags of Danny's torn clothing. "What have you been up to?"

"Please, Bartholomew," Tony pleaded, "he's not well. I tied him up to stop him from hurting himself. Or me."

Tepes laughed. "Pull the other one." He raised Danny's jaw and watched as his head flopped back to his chest. He saw the bong. "No, this is something else. He's under-age, is that it? You one of Cyril's gang?"

Cyril wheeze-laughed against the back of his neck.

"Seems like we're all a bunch of sickos, Cyril." Tepes propped his crutch against the side of the chair and took something from his pocket. He pressed a button, and a blade slid out of a black handle. "I thought I was a goner, but I'm feeling better all the time and I know of a great pick-me-up." He pushed Danny's head back and addressed Cyril. "He's all yours, Cyril, this one is mine." He swooped over Danny, his back blocking the view of whatever he was about to do.

Cyril squeezed his forearm against Tony's throat.

Tony felt the darkness closing in, his whole body becoming leaden.

"Blood," Tepes said, showing Tony the knife pressed against Danny's neck, "is the life."

Tony bucked and brayed in Cyril's arms but it was no good; as the blackness started to overwhelm him, he saw the knife slice across Danny's prominent jugular vein and Tepes press his lips against the spurting red wound.

Epilogue

Seven-and-a-half feet beneath the disturbed earth of Boxford arboretum, something stirred. Microscopical warfare was afoot inside a recently deceased body, which was its battleground. Toxins fought bacteria, viruses, natural chemicals, and the beginning of decomposition, but also against something new. Life, that shouldn't be, rushed to the surface of marbled skin.

She pushed at the soil, panic overwhelming her. She parted her lips to scream and cold earth fell into her mouth. The monstrous strength within ripped her apart and she had no choice as her body crackled and warped into a new structure.

The werewolf pushed itself up out of the ground, grey fur matted down with mud and the blood of change. It collapsed onto the grass, weak, and expelled great mouthfuls of dirt and crawling things. The full moon drenched it in its healing balm and as quickly as it had changed did it metamorphose back into a shivering, naked, elderly woman.

Elizabeth opened her eyes beneath the fat white moon and screamed.

FERAL

Matthew Cash

These stories will continue in
FÜHRER

Coming soon

FERAL

Author Biography

Matthew Cash, or Matty-Bob Cash, as he is known to most, was born and raised in Suffolk, which is the setting for his debut novel, Pinprick. He is compiler and editor of Death by Chocolate, a chocoholic horror anthology, and the 12Days Anthology, head of Burdizzo Books and Burdizzo Bards, and has numerous releases on Kindle and several collections in paperback.

He has always written stories since he first learned to write, and most, although not all, tend to slip into the many-layered murky depths of the Horror genre.

His influences —from childhood to present day— include Roald Dahl, James Herbert, Clive Barker, Stephen King, and Stephen Laws, to name but a few.

More recently, he enjoys the work of Adam Nevill, F.R Tallis, Michael Bray, Gary Fry, William Meikle and Iain Rob Wright (who featured Matty-Bob in his famous A-Z of Horror title, M is For Matty-Bob, plus Matthew wrote his own version of events, which was included as a bonus).

He is a father of two, a husband of one, and a zookeeper of numerous fur babies.

You can find him here:
www.facebook.com/pinprickbymatthewcash
https://www.amazon.co.uk/-/e/B010MQTWKK

FERAL

Other Titles by Matthew Cash

FERAL

Matthew Cash

PINPRICK

All villages have their secrets, and Brantham is no different.

Twenty-years ago, after foolish risk-taking turned into tragedy, Shane left the rural community under a cloud of suspicion and rumour. Events from that night remain unexplained, memories erased, questions unanswered. Now a notorious politician, he returns to his birthplace when the offer from a property developer is too good to refuse. With big plans to haul Brantham into the 21st century, the developers have already made a devastating impact on the once quaint village. But then the headaches begin, followed by the nightmarish visions.

Soon, Shane wishes he had never returned, as Brantham reveals its ugly secret.

FERAL

Matthew Cash

VIRGIN AND THE HUNTER

Hi, I'm God. And I have a confession to make.

I live with my two best friends and the girl of my dreams, Persephone.

When opportunity knocks, we are usually down the pub having a few drinks, or we'll hang out in Christchurch Park until it gets dark, then go home to do college stuff. Even though I struggle a bit financially, life is good, carefree.

Well, it was.

Things have started going downhill recently, from the moment I started killing people.

FERAL

Matthew Cash

KRACKERJACK

Five people wake up in a warehouse, bound to chairs.

Before each of them, tacked to the wall, are their witness testimonies.

They each played a part in labelling one of Britain's most loved family entertainers a paedophile and sex offender.

Clearly, revenge is the reason they have been brought here, but the man they accused is supposed to be dead.

Opportunity knocks, and Diddy Dave Diamond has one last game show to host — and it's a knockout.

FERAL

Matthew Cash

KRACKERJACK2

Ever wondered what would happen if a celebrity faked their own death and decided they had changed their minds?

Two years ago, publicly shunned comedian Diddy Dave Diamond convinced the nation that he was dead, only to return from beyond the grave to seek retribution on those who ruined his career and tainted his legacy.

Innocent or not, only one person survived Diddy Dave Diamond's last ever game show, but the forfeit prize was imprisonment for similar alleged crimes.

Prison is not kind to inmates with those type of convictions, as the sole survivor finds out, but there's a sudden glimmer of hope.

Someone has surfaced in the public eye claiming to be the dead comedian.

FERAL

Matthew Cash

FUR

The old-aged pensioners of Boxford are set in their ways, loyal to each other and their daily routines. With families and loved ones either moved on to pastures new or maybe even the next life, these folk can become dependent on one another.

But what happens when the natural ailments of old age begin to take their toll?

What if they were given the opportunity to heal, and overcome the things that make everyday life less tolerable?

What if they were given this ability without their consent?

When a group of local thugs attack the village's wealthy Victor Krauss, they unwittingly create a maelstrom of events that not only could destroy their home but everyone in and around it.

Are the old folk the cause or the cure of the horrors?

FERAL

Matthew Cash

YOUR FRIGHTFUL SPIRIT STAYED

Something happened deep in Charlie's past to make him the way he is. Something causes the visitations, the disturbances, the ghosts. Is it something in his current life or something from a previous existence? Something haunts Charlie, has followed him for years. Something relentless and unstoppable. Something that only wants to torment, torture and ruin. Something that will chase him to the grave.

FERAL

Matthew Cash

THE GLUT

FREE YOURSELF

What would you do if you found out your compulsions were not your fault?

That something else had been controlling you all along?

What would you do if you discovered there was a dark part of you, a part of humanity, that was put there by an entity older than the stars?

Vince is binge-eating himself into an early grave. He cannot resist the voice inside that encourages him to gorge, an instinctive reaction to every strong emotion. Finding it increasingly more difficult to live with, he vows to do anything to rid himself of it.

Even if it means stooping to new lows and levels of degradation of which he never considered himself capable.

FERAL

Matthew Cash

THE DAY BEFORE YOU CAME

When Philippa spots the bungalow it's love at first sight —and she is filled with the sense of safety and warmth whenever she's there. She's not a believer in the supernatural, unlike her best friend, Niamh, but she has to admit there is an energy about the bungalow, a vibrancy that fills her with joy.

Her boyfriend, Ryan, is an angry waste of space, a compulsive liar and petty criminal. He's not frightened of anything - living or dead.

THIS IS NOT YOUR HOUSE

Roger and Vera have been married for years. Everything is a slog, everything is a burden, to Roger, anyway. Having to spend the majority of his life living with his elderly mother-in-law is enough to make anyone bitter.

Vera puts up with her husband even though he doesn't hear the strange noises in the house.

The everyday tedium continues until Roger devises a way to get rid of his mother-in-law.

FERAL

Other Releases by Matthew Cash

Novels
Virgin and the Hunter
Pinprick
FUR
Your Frightful Spirit Stayed
The Day Before You Came
The Glut

Novellas
Ankle Biters
KrackerJack
KrackerJack 2
Clinton Reed's Fat
Illness
Hell and Sebastian
Waiting for Godfrey
Deadbeard
The Cat Came Back
Frosty

Short Stories
Why Can't I Be You?
Slugs and Snails and Puppydog Tails
OldTimers
Hunt the C*nt
Werwolf

Non-fiction
From Whale-Boy to Aqua-man

FERAL

Anthologies Compiled and Edited by Matthew Cash of Burdizzo Books
Death by Chocolate
12 Days STOCKING FILLERS
12 Days: 2016
12 Days: 2017
The Reverend Burdizzo's Hymnbook*
SPARKS*
Under the Weather [with Em Dehaney & Back Road Books]
Burdizzo Mix Tape Vol.1*
*With Em Dehaney
Corona-Nation Street

Anthologies Featuring Matthew Cash
Rejected for Content 3: Vicious Vengeance
JEApers Creepers
Full Moon Slaughter
Full Moon Slaughter 2
Down the Rabbit Hole: Tales of Insanity
Visions From the Void [edited by Jonathan Butcher & Em Dehaney]

Collections
The Cash Compendium Volume One
The Cash Compendium Continuity
Come and Raise Demons [poetry]
Stromboli and Other Sporadic Eruptions

Website:
www.Facebook.com/pinprickbymatthewcash
Copyright © Matthew Cash 2023